Penguin Books
The Magic Barrel

Bernard Malamud was born in April 1914 in Brooklyn, New York. He took his B.A. degree at the City College of New York and his M.A. at Columbia University. After various odd jobs he began to teach in 1939. He now teaches at Bennington College and lives in Vermont with his wife.

His remarkable first novel, *The Natural*, appeared in 1952. It was followed by *The Assistant* (1957, winner of the Rosenthal Award and the Daroff Memorial Award), *The Magic Barrel* (1958, which won the National Book Award), *A New Life, Idiots First* (1963, short stories) and *Pictures of Fidelman* (1969). *The Fixer*, his fourth novel, was widely praised when it first appeared in 1966 and won him a second National Book Award and a Pulitzer Prize. His later work includes *The Tenants* (1971), *Rembrandt's Hat* (1973, short stories) and *Dubin's Lives* (1979). All these books are published in Penguins.

Bernard Malamud was made a member of the National Institute of Arts and Letters, U.S.A., in 1964 and a member of the American Academy of Arts and Sciences in 1967.

Bernard Malamud

The Magic Barrel

Penguin Books
in association with
Chatto & Windus

Penguin Books Ltd, Harmondsworth,
Middlesex, England
Penguin Books, 625 Madison Avenue,
New York, New York 10022, U.S.A.
Penguin Books Australia Ltd, Ringwood,
Victoria, Australia
Penguin Books Canada Ltd, 2801 John Street,
Markham, Ontario, Canada L3R 1B4
Penguin Books (N.Z.) Ltd, 182-190 Wairau Road,
Auckland 10, New Zealand

First published in the U.S.A. 1958
Published in Great Britain by Eyre & Spottiswoode 1960
Published in Penguin Books 1968
Reprinted 1980

Copyright © Bernard Malamud, 1950, 1951, 1952, 1953,
1954, 1955, 1956, 1958
Copyright © The American Mercury Magazine, 1953
All rights reserved

Made and printed in Great Britain by
C. Nicholls & Company Ltd
Set in Linotype Juliana

For Eugene

Contents

The First Seven Years 9

The Mourners 21

The Girl of My Dreams 30

Angel Levine 43

Behold the Key 55

Take Pity 79

The Prison 88

The Lady of the Lake 95

A Summer's Reading 120

The Bill 129

The Last Mohican 137

The Loan 162

The Magic Barrel 170

The First Seven Years

Feld, the shoemaker, was annoyed that his helper, Sobel, was so insensitive to his reverie that he wouldn't for a minute cease his fanatic pounding at the other bench. He gave him a look, but Sobel's bald head was bent over the last as he worked and he didn't notice. The shoemaker shrugged and continued to peer through the partly frosted window at the near-sighted haze of falling February snow. Neither the shifting white blur outside, nor the sudden deep remembrance of the snowy Polish village where he had wasted his youth could turn his thoughts from Max the college boy (a constant visitor in the mind since early that morning when Feld saw him trudging through the snowdrifts on his way to school), whom he so much respected because of the sacrifices he had made throughout the years – in winter or direst heat – to further his education. An old wish returned to haunt the shoemaker: that he had had a son instead of a daughter, but this blew away in the snow, for Feld, if anything, was a practical man. Yet he could not help but contrast the diligence of the boy, who was a pedlar's son, with Miriam's unconcern for an education. True, she was always with a book in her hand, yet when the opportunity arose for a college education, she had said no she would rather find a job. He had begged her to go, pointing out how many fathers could not afford to send their children to college, but she said she wanted to be independent. As for education, what was it, she asked, but books, which Sobel, who diligently read the classics, would as usual advise her on. Her answer greatly grieved her father.

A figure emerged from the snow and the door opened. At

the counter the man withdrew from a wet paper bag a pair of battered shoes for repair. Who he was the shoemaker for a moment had no idea, then his heart trembled as he realized, before he had thoroughly discerned the face, that Max himself was standing there, embarrassedly explaining what he wanted done to his old shoes. Though Feld listened eagerly, he couldn't hear a word, for the opportunity that had burst upon him was deafening.

He couldn't exactly recall when the thought had occurred to him, because it was clear he had more than once considered suggesting to the boy that he go out with Miriam. But he had not dared speak, for if Max said no, how would he face him again? Or suppose Miriam, who harped so often on independence, blew up in anger and shouted at him for his meddling? Still, the chance was too good to let by: all it meant was an introduction. They might long ago have become friends had they happened to meet somewhere, therefore was it not his duty – an obligation – to bring them together, nothing more, a harmless connivance to replace an accidental encounter in the subway, let's say, or a mutual friend's introduction in the street? Just let him once see and talk to her and he would for sure be interested. As for Miriam, what possible harm for a working girl in an office, who met only loud-mouthed salesmen and illiterate shipping clerks, to make the acquaintance of a fine scholarly boy? Maybe he would awaken in her a desire to go to college; if not – the shoemaker's mind at last came to grips with the truth – let her marry an educated man and live a better life.

When Max finished describing what he wanted done to his shoes, Feld marked them, both with enormous holes in the soles which he pretended not to notice, with large white-chalk x's, and the rubber heels, thinned to the nails, he marked with o's, though it troubled him he might have mixed up the letters. Max inquired the price, and the shoemaker cleared his throat and asked the boy, above Sobel's insistent hammering, would he please step through the side door there into the hall. Though surprised, Max did as the shoemaker requested, and Feld went in after him. For a minute they were both silent, because Sobel had stopped banging, and it seemed they understood neither was to say anything until the noise began again. When it did, loudly, the shoemaker quickly told Max why he had asked to talk to him.

'Ever since you went to high school,' he said, in the dimly-lit hallway, 'I watched you in the morning go to the sub-way to school, and I said always to myself, this is a fine boy that he wants so much an education.'

'Thanks,' Max said, nervously alert. He was tall and gro-tesquely thin, with sharply cut features, particularly a beak-like nose. He was wearing a loose, long slushy overcoat that hung down to his ankles, looking like a rug draped over his bony shoulders, and a soggy, old brown hat, as battered as the shoes he had brought in.

'I am a business man,' the shoemaker abruptly said to con-ceal his embarrassment, 'so I will explain you right away why I talk to you. I have a girl, my daughter Miriam – she is nine-teen – a very nice girl and also so pretty that everybody looks on her when she passes by in the street. She is smart, always with a book, and I thought to myself that a boy like you, an educated boy – I thought maybe you will be interested some-time to meet a girl like this.' He laughed a bit when he had finished and was tempted to say more but had the good sense not to.

Max stared down like a hawk. For an uncomfortable second he was silent, then he asked, 'Did you say nineteen?'

'Yes.'

'Would it be all right to inquire if you have a picture of her?'

'Just a minute.' The shoemaker went into the store and hastily returned with a snapshot that Max held up to the light.

'She's all right,' he said.

Feld waited.

'And is she sensible – not the flighty kind?'

'She is very sensible.'

After another short pause, Max said it was okay with him if he met her.

'Here is my telephone,' said the shoemaker, hurriedly handing him a slip of paper. 'Call her up. She comes home from work six o'clock.'

Max folded the paper and tucked it away into his worn leather wallet.

'About the shoes,' he said. 'How much did you say they will cost me?'

'Don't worry about the price.'

'I just like to have an idea.'

'A dollar – dollar fifty. A dollar fifty,' the shoemaker said.

At once he felt bad, for he usually charged two twenty-five for this kind of job. Either he should have asked the regular price or done the work for nothing.

Later, as he entered the store, he was startled by a violent clanging and looked up to see Sobel pounding with all his might upon the naked last. It broke, the iron striking the floor and jumping with a thump against the wall, but before the enraged shoemaker could cry out, the assistant had torn his hat and coat from the hook and rushed out into the snow.

So Feld, who had looked forward to anticipating how it would go with his daughter and Max, instead had a great worry on his mind. Without his temperamental helper he was a lost man, especially since it was years now that he had carried the store alone. The shoemaker had for an age suffered from a heart condition that threatened collapse if he dared exert himself. Five years ago, after an attack, it had appeared as though he would have either to sacrifice his business upon the auction block and live on a pittance thereafter, or put himself at the mercy of some unscrupulous employee who would in the end probably ruin him. But just at the moment of his darkest despair, this Polish refugee, Sobel, appeared one night from the street and begged for work. He was a stocky man, poorly dressed, with a bald head that had once been blond, a severely plain face and soft blue eyes prone to tears over the sad books he read, a young man but old – no one would have guessed thirty. Though he confessed he knew nothing of shoemaking, he said he was apt and would work for a very little if Feld taught him the trade. Thinking that with, after all, a landsman, he would have less to fear than from a complete stranger, Feld took him on and within six weeks the refugee rebuilt as good a shoe as he, and not long thereafter expertly ran the business for the thoroughly relieved shoemaker.

Feld could trust him with anything and did, frequently going home after an hour or two at the store, leaving all the money in the till, knowing Sobel would guard every cent of it. The amazing thing was that he demanded so little. His wants were few; in money he wasn't interested – in nothing but books, it seemed – which he one by one lent to Miriam, together with his profuse, queer written comments, manufactured during his lonely rooming-house evenings, thick pads of commentary which the shoemaker peered at and twitched his shoulders over as his daughter, from her fourteenth year, read page by sanctified page, as if the word of God were inscribed on them. To protect Sobel, Feld himself had to see that he received more than he asked for. Yet his conscience bothered him for not insisting that the assistant accept a better wage than he was getting, though Feld had honestly told him he could earn a handsome salary if he worked elsewhere, or maybe opened a place of his own. But the assistant answered, somewhat ungraciously, that he was not interested in going elsewhere, and though Feld frequently asked himself what keeps him here? why does he stay? he finally answered it that the man, no doubt because of his terrible experiences as a refugee, was afraid of the world.

After the incident with the broken last, angered by Sobel's behaviour, the shoemaker decided to let him stew for a week in the rooming house, although his own strength was taxed dangerously and the business suffered. However, after several sharp nagging warnings from both his wife and daughter, he went finally in search of Sobel, as he had once before, quite recently, when over some fancied slight – Feld had merely asked him not to give Miriam so many books to read because her eyes were strained and red – the assistant had left the place in a huff, an incident which, as usual, came to nothing for he had returned after the shoemaker had talked to him, and taken his seat at the bench. But this time, after Feld had plodded through the snow to Sobel's house – he had thought of sending Miriam but the idea became repugnant to him – the burly landlady at the door informed him in a nasal voice that Sobel was not at home, and though Feld knew this was a nasty lie, for where had the refugee to go? still for some reason he was not completely sure of – it may have been the cold and his fatigue – he decided not to insist on seeing him. Instead he went home and hired a new helper.

Having settled the matter, though not entirely to his satisfaction, for he had much more to do than before, and so, for example, could no longer lie late in bed mornings because he had to get up to open the store for the new assistant, a speechless, dark man with an irritating rasp as he worked, whom he would not trust with the key as he had Sobel. Furthermore, this one, though able to do a fair repair job, knew nothing of grades of leather or prices, so Feld had to make his own purchases; and every night at closing time it was necessary to count the money in the till and lock up. However, he was not dissatisfied, for he lived much in his thoughts of Max and Miriam. The college boy had called her, and they had arranged a meeting for this coming Friday night. The shoemaker would personally have preferred Saturday, which he felt would make it a date of the first magnitude, but he learned Friday was Miriam's choice, so he said nothing. The day of the week did not matter. What mattered was the aftermath. Would they like each other and want to be friends? He sighed at all the time that would have to go by before he knew for sure. Often he was tempted to talk to Miriam about the boy, to ask whether she thought she would like his type – he had told her only that he considered Max a nice boy and had suggested he call her – but the one time he tried she snapped at him – justly – how should she know?

At last Friday came. Feld was not feeling particularly well so he stayed in bed, and Mrs Feld thought it better to remain in the bedroom with him when Max called. Miriam received the boy, and her parents could hear their voices, his throaty one, as they talked. Just before leaving, Miriam brought Max to the bedroom door and he stood there a minute, a tall, slightly hunched figure wearing a thick, droopy suit, and apparently at ease as he greeted the shoemaker and his wife, which was surely a good sign. And Miriam, although she had worked all day, looked fresh and pretty. She was a large-framed girl with a well-shaped body, and she had a fine open face and soft hair. They made, Feld thought, a first-class couple.

Miriam returned after 11.30. Her mother was already asleep, but the shoemaker got out of bed and after locating his bathrobe went into the kitchen, where Miriam, to his surprise, sat at the table, reading.

'So where did you go?' Feld asked pleasantly.

'For a walk,' she said, not looking up.

'I advised him,' Feld said, clearing his throat, 'he shouldn't spend so much money.'

'I didn't care.'

The shoemaker boiled up some water for tea and sat down at the table with a cupful and a thick slice of lemon.

'So how,' he sighed after a sip, 'did you enjoy?'

'It was all right.'

He was silent. She must have sensed his disappointment, for she added, 'You can't really tell much the first time.'

'You will see him again?'

Turning a page, she said that Max had asked for another date.

'For when?'

'Saturday.'

'So what did you say?'

'What did I say?' she asked, delaying for a moment – 'I said yes.'

Afterwards she inquired about Sobel, and Feld, without exactly knowing why, said the assistant had got another job. Miriam said nothing more and began to read. The shoemaker's conscience did not trouble him; he was satisfied with the Saturday date.

During the week, by placing here and there a deft question, he managed to get from Miriam some information about Max. It surprised him to learn that the boy was not studying to be either a doctor or lawyer but was taking a business course leading to a degree in accountancy. Feld was a little disappointed because he thought of accountants as book-keepers and would have preferred 'a higher profession'. However, it was not long before he had investigated the subject and discovered that Certified Public Accountants were highly respected people, so he was thoroughly content as Saturday approached. But because Saturday was a busy day, he was much in the store and therefore did not see Max when he came to call for Miriam. From his wife he learned there had been nothing especially revealing about their meeting. Max had rung the bell and Miriam had got her coat and left with him – nothing more. Feld did not probe, for his wife was not particularly observant. Instead, he waited up for Miriam with a newspaper on his lap, which he scarcely looked at so lost was he in thinking of the future. He awoke to find her in the room with him, tiredly removing her hat. Greeting her, he was suddenly inexplicably afraid to ask anything about the evening. But since she volunteered nothing he was at last forced to inquire how she had enjoyed herself. Miriam began something non-committal but apparently changed her mind, for she said after a minute, 'I was bored.'

When Feld had sufficiently recovered from his anguished disappointment to ask why, she answered without hesitation, 'Because he's nothing more than a materialist.'

'What means this word?'

'He has no soul. He's only interested in things.'

He considered her statement for a long time but then asked, 'Will you see him again?'

'He didn't ask.'

'Suppose he will ask you?'

'I won't see him.'

He did not argue; however, as the days went by he hoped increasingly she would change her mind. He wished the boy would telephone, because he was sure there was more to him than Miriam, with her inexperienced eye, could discern. But Max didn't call. As a matter of fact he took a different route to school, no longer passing the shoemaker's store, and Feld was deeply hurt.

Then one afternoon Max came in and asked for his shoes. The shoemaker took them down from the shelf where he had placed them, apart from the other pairs. He had done the work himself and the soles and heels were well built and firm. The shoes had been highly polished and somehow looked better than new. Max's Adam's apple went up once when he saw them, and his eyes had little lights in them.

'How much?' he asked, without directly looking at the shoemaker.

'Like I told you before,' Feld answered sadly. 'One dollar fifty cents.'

Max handed him two crumpled bills and received in return a newly-minted silver half dollar.

He left. Miriam had not been mentioned. That night the shoemaker discovered that his new assistant had been all the while stealing from him, and he suffered a heart attack.

Though the attack was very mild, he lay in bed for three weeks. Miriam spoke of going for Sobel, but sick as he was Feld rose in wrath against the idea. Yet in his heart he knew there was no other way, and the first weary day back in the shop thoroughly convinced him, so that night after supper he dragged himself to Sobel's rooming house.

He toiled up the stairs, though he knew it was bad for him, and at the top knocked at the door. Sobel opened it and the shoemaker entered. The room was a small, poor one, with a single window facing the street. It contained a narrow cot, a low table and several stacks of books piled haphazardly around on the floor along the wall, which made him think how queer Sobel was, to be uneducated and read so much. He had once asked him, Sobel, why you read so much? and the assistant could not answer him. Did you ever study in a college some-place? he had asked, but Sobel shook his head. He read, he said, to know. But to know what, the shoemaker demanded, and to know, why? Sobel never explained, which proved he read much because he was queer.

Feld sat down to recover his breath. The assistant was rest-ing on his bed with his heavy back to the wall. His shirt and trousers were clean, and his stubby fingers, away from the shoemaker's bench, were strangely pallid. His face was thin and pale, as if he had been shut in this room since the day he had bolted from the store.

'So when you will come back to work?' Feld asked him.

To his surprise, Sobel burst out, 'Never.'

Jumping up, he strode over to the window that looked out upon the miserable street. 'Why should I come back?' he cried.

'I will raise your wages.'

'Who cares for your wages!'

The shoemaker, knowing he didn't care, was at a loss what else to say.

'What do you want from me, Sobel?'

'Nothing.'

'I always treated you like you was my son.'

Sobel vehemently denied it. 'So why you look for strange boys in the street they should go out with Miriam? Why you don't think of me?'

The shoemaker's hands and feet turned freezing cold. His voice became so hoarse he couldn't speak. At last he cleared his throat and croaked, 'So what has my daughter got to do with a shoemaker thirty-five years old who works for me?'

'Why do you think I worked so long for you?' Sobel cried out. 'For the stingy wages I sacrificed five years of my life so you could have to eat and drink and where to sleep?'

'Then for what?' shouted the shoemaker.

'For Miriam,' he blurted – 'for her.'

The shoemaker, after a time, managed to say, 'I pay wages in cash, Sobel,' and lapsed into silence. Though he was seething with excitement, his mind was coldly clear, and he had to admit to himself he had sensed all along that Sobel felt this way. He had never so much as thought it consciously, but he had felt it and was afraid.

'Miriam knows?' he muttered hoarsely.

'She knows.'

'You told her?'

'No.'

'Then how does she know?'

'How does she know?' Sobel said, 'because she knows. She knows who I am and what is in my heart.'

Feld had a sudden insight. In some devious way, with his books and commentary, Sobel had given Miriam to understand that he loved her. The shoemaker felt a terrible anger at him for his deceit.

'Sobel, you are crazy,' he said bitterly. 'She will never marry a man so old and ugly like you.'

Sobel turned black with rage. He cursed the shoemaker, but then, though he trembled to hold it in, his eyes filled with tears and he broke into deep sobs. With his back to Feld, he stood at the window, fists clenched, and his shoulders shook with his choked sobbing.

Watching him, the shoemaker's anger diminished. His teeth were on edge with pity for the man, and his eyes grew moist. How strange and sad that a refugee, a grown man, bald and old with his miseries, who had by the skin of his teeth escaped Hitler's incinerators, should fall in love, when he had got to America, with a girl less than half his age. Day after day, for five years he had sat at his bench, cutting and hammering away, waiting for the girl to become a woman, unable to ease his heart with speech, knowing no protest but desperation.

'Ugly I didn't mean,' he said half aloud.

Then he realized that what he had called ugly was not Sobel but Miriam's life if she married him. He felt for his daughter a strange and gripping sorrow, as if she were already Sobel's bride, the wife, after all, of a shoemaker, and had in her life no more than her mother had had. And all his dreams for her – why he had slaved and destroyed his heart with anxiety and labour – all these dreams of a better life were dead.

The room was quiet. Sobel was standing by the window reading, and it was curious that when he read he looked young.

'She is only nineteen,' Feld said brokenly. 'This is too young yet to get married. Don't ask her for two years more, till she is twenty-one, then you can talk to her.'

Sobel didn't answer. Feld rose and left. He went slowly down the stairs but once outside, though it was an icy night and the crisp falling snow whitened the street, he walked with a stronger stride.

But the next morning, when the shoemaker arrived, heavy-hearted, to open the store, he saw he needn't have come, for his assistant was already seated at the last, pounding leather for his love.

The Mourners

Kessler, formerly an egg candler, lived alone on social security. Though past sixty-five, he might have found well-paying work with more than one butter and egg wholesaler, for he sorted and graded with speed and accuracy, but he was a quarrelsome type and considered a trouble maker, so the wholesalers did without him. Therefore, after a time he retired, living with few wants on his old-age pension. Kessler inhabited a small cheap flat on the top floor of a decrepit tenement on the East Side. Perhaps because he lived above so many stairs, no one bothered to visit him. He was much alone, as he had been most of his life. At one time he'd had a family, but unable to stand his wife or children, always in his way, he had after some years walked out on them. He never saw them thereafter, because he never sought them, and they did not seek him. Thirty years had passed. He had no idea where they were, nor did he think much about it.

In the tenement, although he had lived there ten years, he was more or less unknown. The tenants on both sides of his flat on the fifth floor, an Italian family of three middle-aged sons and their wizened mother, and a sullen, childless German couple named Hoffman, never said hello to him, nor did he greet any of them on the way up or down the narrow wooden stairs. Others of the house recognized Kessler when they passed him in the street, but they thought he lived elsewhere on the block. Ignace, the small, bent-back janitor, knew him best, for they had several times played two-handed pinochle; but Ignace, usually the loser because he lacked skill at cards, had stopped going up after a time. He complained to his wife that he couldn't stand the stink there, that the filthy flat with its junky furniture made him sick. The janitor had spread the word about Kessler to the others on the floor, and they shunned him as a dirty old man. Kessler understood this but had contempt for them all.

One day Ignace and Kessler began a quarrel over the way the egg candler piled oily bags overflowing with garbage into the dumb-waiter, instead of using a pail. One word shot off another, and they were soon calling each other savage names, when Kessler slammed the door in the janitor's face. Ignace ran down five flights of stairs and loudly cursed out the old man to his impassive wife. It happened that Gruber, the land-lord, a fat man with a consistently worried face, who wore yards of baggy clothes, was in the building, making a check of plumbing repairs, and to him the enraged Ignace related the trouble he was having with Kessler. He described, holding his nose, the smell in Kessler's flat, and called him the dirtiest person he had ever seen. Gruber knew his janitor was exaggerating, but he felt burdened by financial worries which shot his blood pressure up to astonishing heights, so he settled it quickly by saying, 'Give him notice.' None of the tenants in the house had held a written lease since the war, and Gruber felt confident, in case somebody asked questions, that he could easily justify his dismissal of Kessler as an undesirable tenant. It had occurred to him that Ignace could then slap a cheap coat of paint on the walls and the flat would be let to someone for five dollars more than the old man was paying.

That night after supper, Ignace victoriously ascended the stairs and knocked on Kessler's door. The egg candler opened it, and seeing who stood there, immediately slammed it shut. Ignace shouted through the door, 'Mr Gruber says to give notice. We don't want you around here. Your dirt stinks the whole house.' There was silence, but Ignace waited, relishing what he had said. Although after five minutes he still heard no sound, the janitor stayed there, picturing the old Jew trembling behind the locked door. He spoke again, 'You got two weeks' notice till the first, then you better move out or Mr Gruber and myself will throw you out.' Ignace watched as the door slowly opened. To his surprise he found himself frightened at the old man's appearance. He looked, in the act of opening the door, like a corpse adjusting his coffin lid. But if he appeared dead, his voice was alive. It rose terrifyingly harsh from his throat, and he sprayed curses over all the years of Ignace's life. His eyes were reddened, his cheeks sunken, and his wisp of beard moved agitatedly. He seemed to be losing weight as he shouted. The janitor no longer had any heart for the matter, but he could not bear so many insults all at once so he cried out, 'You dirty old bum, you better get out and don't make so much trouble.' To this the enraged Kessler swore they would first have to kill him and drag him out dead.

On the morning of the first of December, Ignace found in his letter box a soiled folded paper containing Kessler's twenty-five dollars. He showed it to Gruber that evening when the landlord came to collect the rent money. Gruber, after a minute of absently contemplating the money, frowned disgustedly.

'I thought I told you to give notice.'

'Yes, Mr Gruber,' Ignace agreed. 'I gave him.'

'That's a helluva chuzpah,' said Gruber. 'Gimme the keys.'

Ignace brought the ring of pass keys, and Gruber, breathing heavily, began the lumbering climb up the long avenue of stairs. Although he rested on each landing, the fatigue of climbing, and his profuse flowing perspiration, heightened his irritation.

Arriving at the top floor he banged his fist on Kessler's door. 'Gruber, the landlord. Open up here.'

There was no answer, no movement within, so Gruber inserted the key into the lock and twisted. Kessler had barricaded the door with a chest and some chairs. Gruber had to put his shoulder to the door and shove before he could step into the hallway of the badly-lit two and a half room flat. The old man, his face drained of blood, was standing in the kitchen doorway.

'I warned you to scram outa here,' Gruber said loudly. 'Move out or I'll telephone the city marshal.'

'Mr Gruber –' began Kessler.

'Don't bother me with your lousy excuses, just beat it.' He gazed around. 'It looks like a junk shop and it smells like a toilet. It'll take me a month to clean up here.'

'This smell is only cabbage that I am cooking for my supper. Wait, I'll open a window and it will go away.'

'When you go away, it'll go away.' Gruber took out his bulky wallet, counted out twelve dollars, added fifty cents, and plunked the money on top of the chest. 'You got two more weeks till the fifteenth, then you gotta be out or I will get a dispossess. Don't talk back talk. Get outa here and go somewhere that they don't know you and maybe you'll get a place.'

'No, Mr Gruber,' Kessler cried passionately. 'I didn't do nothing, and I will stay here.'

'Don't monkey with my blood pressure,' said Gruber. 'If you're not out by the fifteenth, I will personally throw you on your bony ass.'

Then he left and walked heavily down the stairs.

The fifteenth came and Ignace found the twelve fifty in his letter box. He telephoned Gruber and told him.

'I'll get a dispossess,' Gruber shouted. He instructed the janitor to write out a note saying to Kessler that his money was refused and to stick it under his door. This Ignace did. Kessler returned the money to the letter box, but again Ignace wrote a note and slipped it, with the money, under the old man's door.

After another day Kessler received a copy of his eviction notice. It said to appear in court on Friday at 10 a.m. to show cause why he should not be evicted for continued neglect and destruction of rental property. The official notice filled Kessler with great fright because he had never in his life been to court. He did not appear on the day he had been ordered to.

That same afternoon the marshal appeared with two brawny assistants. Ignace opened Kessler's lock for them and as they pushed their way into the flat, the janitor hastily ran down the stairs to hide in the cellar. Despite Kessler's wailing and carrying on, the two assistants methodically removed his meagre furniture and set it out on the sidewalk. After that they got Kessler out, though they had to break open the bathroom door because the old man had locked himself in there. He shouted, struggled, pleaded with his neighbours to help him, but they looked on in a silent group outside the door. The two assistants, holding the old man tightly by the arms and skinny legs, carried him kicking and moaning, down the stairs. They sat him in the street on a chair amid his junk. Upstairs, the marshal bolted the door with a lock Ignace had supplied, signed a paper which he handed to the janitor's wife, and then drove off in an automobile with his assistants.

Kessler sat on a split chair on the sidewalk. It was raining and the rain soon turned to sleet, but he still sat there. People passing by skirted the pile of his belongings. They stared at Kessler and he stared at nothing. He wore no hat or coat, and the snow fell on him, making him look like a piece of his dispossessed goods. Soon the wizened Italian woman from the top floor returned to the house with two of her sons, each carrying a loaded shopping bag. When she recognized Kessler sitting amid his furniture, she began to shriek. She shrieked in Italian at Kessler although he paid no attention to her. She stood on the stoop, shrunken, gesticulating with thin arms, her loose mouth working angrily. Her sons tried to calm her, but still she shrieked. Several of the neighhbours came down to see who was making the racket. Finally, the two sons, unable to think what else to do, set down their shopping bags, lifted Kessler out of the chair, and carried him up the stairs. Hoffman, Kessler's other neighbour, working with a small triangular file, cut open the padlock, and Kessler was carried into the flat from which he had been evicted. Ignace screeched at everybody, calling them filthy names, but the three men went downstairs and hauled up Kessler's chairs, his broken table, chest, and ancient metal bed. They piled all the furniture into the bedroom. Kessler sat on the edge of the bed and wept. After a while, after the old Italian woman had sent in a soup plate full of hot macaroni seasoned with tomato sauce and grated cheese, they left.

Ignace phoned Gruber. The landlord was eating and the food turned to lumps in his throat. 'I'll throw them all out, the bastards,' he yelled. He put on his hat, got into his car and drove through the slush to the tenement. All the time he was thinking of his worries: high repair costs; it was hard to keep the place together; maybe the building would someday collapse. He had read of such things. All of a sudden the front of the building parted from the rest and fell like a breaking wave into the street. Gruber cursed the old man for taking him from his supper. When he got to the house he snatched Ignace's keys and ascended the sagging stairs. Ignace tried to follow, but Gruber told him to stay the hell in his hole. When the landlord was not looking, Ignace crept up after him.

Gruber turned the key and let himself into Kessler's dark flat. He pulled the light chain and found the old man sitting limply on the side of the bed. On the floor at his feet lay a plate of stiffened macaroni.

'What do you think you're doing here?' Gruber thundered.

The old man sat motionless.

'Don't you know it's against the law? This is trespassing and you're breaking the law. Answer me.'

Kessler remained mute.

Gruber mopped his brow with a large yellowed handkerchief.

'Listen, my friend, you're gonna make lots of trouble for yourself. If they catch you in here you might go to the workhouse. I'm only trying to advise you.'

To his surprise Kessler looked at him with wet, brimming eyes.

'What did I did to you?' he bitterly wept. 'Who throws out of his house a man that he lived there ten years and pays every month on time his rent? What did I do, tell me? Who hurts a man without a reason? Are you a Hitler or a Jew?' He was hitting his chest with his fist.

Gruber removed his hat. He listened carefully, at first at a loss what to say, but then answered: 'Listen, Kessler, it's not personal. I own this house and it's falling apart. My bills are sky high. If the tenants don't take care they have to go. You don't take care and you fight with my janitor, so you have to go. Leave in the morning, and I won't say another word. But if you don't leave the flat, you'll get the heave-ho again. I'll call the marshal.'

'Mr Gruber,' said Kessler, 'I won't go. Kill me if you want it, but I won't go.'

Ignace hurried away from the door as Gruber left in anger. The next morning, after a restless night of worries, the landlord set out to drive to the city marshal's office. On the way he stopped at a candy store for a pack of cigarettes, and there decided once more to speak to Kessler. A thought had occurred to him: he would offer to get the old man into a public home.

He drove to the tenement and knocked on Ignace's door.

'Is the old gink still up there?'

'I don't know if so, Mr Gruber.' The janitor was ill at ease.

'What do you mean you don't know?'

'I didn't see him go out. Before, I looked in his keyhole but nothing moves.'

'So why didn't you open the door with your key?'

'I was afraid,' Ignace answered nervously.

'What are you afraid?'

Ignace wouldn't say.

A fright went through Gruber but he didn't show it. He grabbed the keys and walked ponderously up the stairs, hurrying every so often.

No one answered his knock. As he unlocked the door he broke into heavy sweat.

But the old man was there, alive, sitting without shoes on the bedroom floor.

'Listen, Kessler,' said the landlord, relieved although his head pounded. 'I got an idea that, if you do it the way I say, your troubles are over.'

He explained his proposal to Kessler, but the egg candler

was not listening. His eyes were downcast, and his body swayed slowly sideways. As the landlord talked on, the old man was thinking of what had whirled through his mind as he had sat out on the sidewalk in the falling snow. He had thought through his miserable life, remembering how, as a young man, he had abandoned his family, walking out on his wife and three innocent children, without even in some way attempting to provide for them; without, in all the intervening years – so God help him – once trying to discover if they were alive or dead. How, in so short a life, could a man do so much wrong? This thought smote him to the heart and he recalled the past without end and moaned and tore at his flesh with his fingernails.

Gruber was frightened at the extent of Kessler's suffering. Maybe I should let him stay, he thought. Then as he watched the old man, he realized he was bunched up there on the floor engaged in an act of mourning. There he sat, white from fasting, rocking back and forth, his beard dwindled to a shade of itself.

Something's wrong here – Gruber tried to imagine what and found it all oppressive. He felt he ought to run out, get away, but then saw himself fall and go tumbling down the five flights of stairs; he groaned at the broken picture of himself lying at the bottom. Only he was still there in Kessler's bedroom, listening to the old man praying. Somebody's dead, Gruber muttered. He figured Kessler had got bad news, yet instinctively knew he hadn't. Then it struck him with a terrible force that the mourner was mourning him: it was *he* who was dead.

The landlord was agonized. Sweating brutally, he felt an enormous constricted weight in him that slowly forced itself up, until his head was at the point of bursting. For a full minute he awaited a stroke; but the feeling painfully passed, leaving him miserable.

When after a while, he gazed around the room, it was clean, drenched in daylight and fragrance. Gruber then suffered unbearable remorse for the way he had treated the old man.

At last he could stand it no longer. With a cry of shame he tore the sheet off Kessler's bed, and wrapping it around his bulk, sank heavily to the floor and became a mourner.

The Girl of My Dreams

After Mitka had burned the manuscript of his heart-broken
novel in the blackened bottom of Mrs Lutz's rusty trash can
in her back yard, although the emotional landlady tried all
sorts of bait and schemes to lure him forth, and he could tell as
he lay abed, from the new sounds on the floor and her pene-
trating perfume, that there was an unattached female loose
on the premises (wondrous possibility of yore), he resisted all
and with a twist of the key had locked himself a prisoner in
his room, only venturing out after midnight for crackers and
tea and an occasional can of fruit; and this went on for too
many weeks to count.

In the late fall, after a long year and a half of voyaging
among more than twenty publishers, the novel had returned
to stay and he had hurled it into a barrel burning autumn
leaves, stirring the mess with a long length of pipe, to get the
inner sheets afire. Overhead a few dead apples hung like forgotten Christmas ornaments upon the leafless tree. The
sparks, as he stirred, flew to the apples, the withered fruit
representing not only creation gone for nothing (three long
years), but all his hopes, and the proud ideas he had given his
book; and Mitka, although not a sentimentalist, felt as if he
had burned (it took a thick two hours) an everlasting hollow in himself.

Into the fire also went a sheaf of odd-size papers (why he
had saved them he would never know): copies of letters to
literary agents and their replies; mostly, however, printed re-
jection forms, with perhaps three typed notes from lady
editors, saying they were returning the MS of his novel,
among other reasons – but this prevailed – because of the

symbolism, the fact that it was obscure. Only one of the
ladies had written let's hear from you again. Though he
cursed them to damnation it did not cause the acceptance of
his book. Yet for a year Mitka laboured over a new one, up to
the time of the return of the old manuscript, when, upon re-
reading that, then the new work, he discovered the same symbolism, more obscure than ever; so he shoved the second book
aside. True, at odd moments he sneaked out of bed to try a
new thought with his pen, but the words refused to budge;
besides he had lost the belief that anything he said could
make significant meaning, and if it perhaps did, that it could
be conveyed in all its truth and drama to some publisher's
reader in his aseptic office high above Madison Avenue; so he
wrote nothing for months – although Mrs Lutz actively
mourned – and vowed never to write again though he felt the
vow was worthless, because he couldn't write anyway whether
he had vowed or no.

So Mitka sat alone and still in his faded yellow-papered
room, the badly coloured Orozco reproduction he had picked
up, showing Mexican peasants bent and suffering, thumb-
tacked above the peeling mantelpiece, and stared through sore
eyes at the antics of pigeons on the roof across the street; or
aimlessly followed traffic – not people – in the street; he slept
for good or ill a great deal, had bad dreams, some horrific, and
awaking, looked long at the ceiling, which never represented
the sky although he imagined it snowing; listened to music if it
came from the distance, and occasionally attempted to read
some historical or philosophical work but shut it with a bang
if it lit the imagination and made him think of writing. At
times he cautioned himself, Mitka, this will have to end or
you will, but the warning did not change his ways. He grew
wan and thin, and once when he beheld his meagre thighs as
he dressed, if he were a weeper he would have wept.

Now Mrs Lutz, herself a writer – a bad one but always
interested in writers and had them in her house whenever she
could fish one up (her introductory inquisition masterfully

sniffed this fact among the first) even when she could ill afford it – Mrs Lutz knew all this about Mitka and she daily attempted some unsuccessful ministration. She tried tempting him down to her kitchen with spry descriptions of lunch: steaming soup, Mitka, with soft white rolls, calf's foot jelly, rice with tomato sauce, celery hearts, delicious breast of chicken – beef if he preferred – and his choice of satisfying sweets; also with fat notes slipped under his door in sealed envelopes, describing when she was a little girl, and the intimate details of her sad life since with Mr Lutz, imploring a better fate on Mitka; or she left at the door all sorts of books fished out of her ancient library that he never looked at, magazines with stories marked, 'You can do better,' and when it arrived, her own copy, for him to read first, of the *Writer's Journal*. All these attempts having this day failed – his door shut (Mitka voiceless) though she had hid in the hall an hour to await its opening – Mrs. Lutz dropped to one horsy knee and with her keyhole eye peeked in: he lay outstretched in bed.

'Mitka,' she wailed, 'how thin you have grown – a skeleton – it frightens me. Come downstairs and eat.'

He remained motionless, so she enticed him otherwise: 'Here are clean sheets on my arm, let me refresh your bed and air the room.'

He groaned for her to go away.

Mrs Lutz groped a minute. 'We have with us a new guest on your floor, girl by the name of Beatrice – a real beauty, Mitka, and a writer too.'

He was silent but, she knew, listening.

'I'd say a tender twenty-one or -two, pinched waist, firm breasts, pretty face, and you should see her little panties hanging on the line – like flowers all.'

'What does she write?' he solemnly inquired.

Mrs Lutz found herself coughing.

'Advertising copy, as I understand, but she would like to write verse.'

He turned away, wordless.

She left a tray in the hall – a bowl of hot soup whose odour nearly drove him mad, two folded sheets, pillow case, fresh towels, and a copy of that morning's *Globe*.

After he had ravished the soup and all but chewed the linen, he tore open the *Globe* to confirm that he was missing nothing. The headlines told him : correct. He was about to crumple the paper and pitch it out the window when he recalled 'The Open Globe' on the editorial page, a column he hadn't looked at in years. In the past he had reached for the paper with five cents and trembling fingers, for 'The Open Globe', come-one, come-all to the public, to every writer under a rock, inviting contributions in the form of stories at five bucks the thousand-word throw. Though he now hated the memory of it, it was his repeated acceptance here – a dozen stories in less than half a year (he had bought a blue suit and a two-pound jar of jam) – that had started him writing the novel (requiescat); from that to the second abortion, to the impotence and murderous self-hatred that had descended upon him afterwards. Open Globe, indeed. He gnashed his teeth but the holes in them hurt. Yet the not unsweet remembrance of past triumphs – the quarter of a million potential readers every time he appeared in print, all within a single city so that *everybody* knew when he was in (people reading him in buses, at cafeteria tables, park benches, as Mitka the Magician lurked around, watching for smiles and tears); also flattering letters from publishers' editors, fan letters too, from the most unlikely people – fame is the purr, the yip the yay. Remembering, he cast a momentarily dewy eye upon the column, and having done so, devoured the print.

The story socked in the belly. This girl, Madeleine Thorn, who wrote the piece as 'I' – though she only traced herself here and there she came at once alive to him – he pictured her as maybe twenty-three, slim yet soft-bodied, the face whiplashed with understanding – that Thorn was not for nothing; anyway, there she was that day, running up and down the stairs in joy and terror. She too lived in a rooming house, at

work on her novel, bit by bit, nights, after a depleting secre-
tarial grind each day; page by page, each neatly typed and
slipped into the carton under her bed. At the very end of the
book a last chapter to go of the first draft, she had one night
got out the carton and lay on the bed, rereading, to see if the
book was any good. Page after page she dropped on the floor, at
last falling asleep, worried she hadn't got it right, wearied at
how much rewriting (this sank in by degrees) she would have
to do, when the light of the risen sun struck her eyes and she
pounced up, realizing she had forgotten to set the alarm.
With a sweep of the hand she shot the typewritten sheets
under the bed, washed, slipped on a fresh dress, and ran a comb
through her hair. Down the stairs she ran and out of the
house.

At work, strangely a good day. The novel again came together in the mind and she memo'd what she'd have to do –
not very much really, to make it the decent book she had
hoped to write. Home, happy, holding flowers, to be met on
the first floor by the landlady, flouncing and all smiles : guess
what I've gone and done for you today; describing new curtains, matching bedspread, a rug no less, to keep your tootsies
warm, and surprise ! the room spring-cleaned from top to bottom. Oh my God. The girl tore up the stairs. Falling on her
hands and knees in her room she searched under the bed : an
empty carton. Downstairs like dark light. Where, landlady,
are the typewritten papers that were under my bed? She spoke
with her hand to her throat. 'Oh, those that I found on the
floor, honey? I thought you meant for me to sweep the mess
out and so I did.' Madeleine, controlling her voice : 'Are they
perhaps in the garbage? I – don't believe they collect it till
Thursday.' 'No, love, I burned them in the barrel this morning. The smoke made my eyes smart for a whole hour.' Curtain. Groaning, Mitka collapsed on the bed.

He was convinced it was every bit of it true. He saw the
crazy dame dumping the manuscript into the barrel and stirring it until every blessed page was aflame. He groaned at the

burning – years of precious work. The tale haunted him. He wanted to escape it – leave the room and abandon the dismal memory of misery, but where would he go and what do without a penny in his pocket? So he lay on the bed and whether awake or asleep dreamed the recurrent dream of the burning barrel (in it their books commingled), suffering her agony as well as his own. The barrel, a symbol he had not conceived before, belched flame, shot word-sparks, poured smoke as thick as oil. It turned red hot, a sickly yellow, black – loaded high with the ashes of human bones – guess whose. When his imagination calmed, a sorrow for her afflicted him. The last chapter – irony of it. He yearned all day to assuage her grief, express sympathy in some loving word or gesture, assure her she would write it again, only better. Around midnight he could bear his thoughts no longer. He thrust a sheet of paper into the portable, twirled the roller and in the strange stillness of the house clacked out to her a note c/o *Globe*, expressing his sorrow – a writer himself – but don't give up, write it again. Sincerely, Mitka. He found an envelope and sticky stamp in his desk drawer. Against his better judgement he sneaked out and mailed it.

Immediately he regretted it. Was he in his right mind? *All right*, so he had written to her, but what if she wrote back? Who wanted, who needed a correspondence? He simply hadn't the strength for it. Therefore he was glad there continued to be no mail – not since he had burned his book in November, and this was February. Yet on the way out to forage some food for himself when the house was sleeping, ridiculing himself, holding a lit match he peered into the mailbox. The next night he felt inside the slot with his fingers: empty, served him right. Silly business. He had all but forgotten her story; that is, thought of it less each day. Yet if the girl by some mischance should write, Mrs Lutz usually opened the box and brought up whatever mail herself – any excuse to waste his time. The next morning he heard the courier carrying her bulk lightly up the stairs and knew the girl had answered. Steady, Mitka. Despite a warning to himself of the dream world he was in, his heart pounded as the old tease coyly knocked. He didn't answer. Gurgling, 'For you, Mitka darling,' she at last slipped it under the door – her favourite pastime. Waiting till she had moved on so as not to give her the satisfaction of hearing him go for it, he sprang off the bed and tore the envelope open. 'Dear Mr Mitka (a most feminine handwriting). Thank you for the expression of your kind sympathy, sincerely, M.T.' That was all, no return address, no nothing. Giving himself a horse bray he dropped the business into the basket. He brayed louder the next day : there was another epistle, the story wasn't true – she had invented every word; but the truth was she was lonely and would he care to write again?

Nothing comes easy for Mitka but eventually he wrote to her. He had plenty of time and nothing else to do. He told himself he had answered her letter because she was lonely – all right, because they both were. Ultimately he admitted that he wrote because he couldn't do the other kind of writing, and this, though he was no escapist, solaced him a bit. Mitka sensed that although he had vowed never to go back to it, he hoped the correspondence would return him to his abandoned book. (Sterile writer seeking end of sterility through satisfying epistolary intercourse with lady writer.) Clearly then, he was trying with these letters to put an end to the hatred of self for not working, for having no ideas, for cutting himself off from them. Ah, Mitka. He sighed at this weakness, to depend on others. Yet though his letters were often harsh, provocative, even unkind, they drew from her warm responses, receptive, soft, willing; and so it was not long (who can resist it? he bitterly assailed himself) before he had brought up the subject of their meeting. He broached it first and she (with reluctance) gave in, for wasn't it better, she had asked, not to intrude the person?

The meeting was arranged for a Monday evening at the branch public library near where she worked – her bookish preference; himself, he would have chosen the freedom of a street corner. She would, she said, be wearing a sort of reddish babushka. Now Mitka found himself actively wondering what she looked like. Her letters showed her sensible, modest, honest but what of the human body? Though he liked his women, among other things, to be lookers, he guessed she wasn't. Partly from hints dropped by her, partly his intuition. He pictured her as comely yet hefty. But what of it as long as she was womanly, intelligent, brave? A man like him nowadays had need of something special.

The March evening was zippy outside but cupped in it the breath of spring. Mitka opened both windows and allowed the free air to blow on him. About to go – there came a quick knock on the door. 'Telephone,' a girl's voice sang out. Probably the advertising Beatrice. He waited till she was gone, then unlocked the door and stepped into the hall for his first phone call of the year. As he picked up the receiver a crack of light showed in the corner. He stared and the door shut tight. The landlady's fault, she built him up among the roomers as a sort of freak. 'My writer upstairs.'

'Mitka?' It was Madeleine.

'Speaking.'

'Mitka, do you know why I'm calling?'

'How should I know?'

'I'm half drunk on wine.'

'Save it till later.'

'Because I am afraid.'

'Afraid of what?'

'I do so love your letters and would hate to lose them. Do we have to meet?'

'Yes,' he hissed.

'Suppose I am not what you expect?'

'Leave that to me.'

She sighed. 'All right then –'

'You'll be there?'

No sound from her.

'For God's sake, don't frustrate me now.'

'Yes, Mitka.' She hung up.

Sensitive kid. He plucked his very last buck out of the drawer and quickly left the room, to hurry to the library before she could change her mind and leave. But Mrs Lutz, in flannel bathrobe, caught him at the bottom of the stairs. Her grey hair wild, her voice broken. 'Mitka, why have you shunned me so long? I have waited months for a single word. How can you be so cruel?'

'Please.' He shoved her aside and ran out of the house. Nutty dame. The balmy current in the air swept away the unpleasantness, carried a sob to his throat. He walked briskly, more alive than for many a season.

The library was an old stone structure. He searched in circulation amid rows of books on sagging floors but found only the yawning librarian. The children's room was dark. In reference, a lone middle-aged female sat at a long table, reading; on the table stood her bulky market bag. Mitka searched the room and was turning to look elsewhere when a monstrous insight tore at his scalp: *this was she.* He stared unbelievingly, his heart a dishrag. Rage possessed him. Hefty she was but yes, eyeglassed, and marvellously plain; Christ, didn't know colour even – the babushka a sickly running orange. Ah, colossal trickery – was ever man so cruelly defrauded? His impulse was to escape into breathable air but she held him there by serenely reading the printed page – (sly one, she knew the tiger in the room). Had she for a split second gazed up with wavering lids he'd have bolted sure; instead she buttoned her eyes to the book and let him duck if he so willed. This infuriated him further. Who wanted charity from the old girl? Mitka strode (in misery) towards her table.

'Madeleine?' He mocked the name. (Writer maims bird in flight. Enough not enough.)

She looked up with a shy and stricken smile. 'Mitka?'

'The same –' He cynically bowed.

'Madeleine is my daughter's name, which I borrowed for my story. Mine is Olga really.'

A pox on her lies – yet he hopefully asked, 'Did she send you?'

She smiled sadly. 'No, I am the one. Sit, Mitka.'

He sat sullenly, harbouring murderous thoughts: to hack her to pieces and incinerate the remains in Mrs Lutz's barrel.

'They'll be closing soon,' she said. 'Where shall we go?'

He was motionless, stunned.

'I know a beer place around the corner where we can refresh ourselves,' Olga suggested.

She buttoned a drab coat over a grey sweater. At length he rose. She got up too and followed him, hauling her market bag down the stone steps.

In the street he took the bag – it felt full of rocks – and trailed her around the corner into the beer joint.

Along the wall opposite the beat-up bar ran a row of dark booths. Olga sought one in the rear.

'For peace and privacy.'

He laid the bag on the table. 'The place smells.'

They sat facing each other. He grew increasingly depressed at the thought of spending the evening with her. The irony of it – immured for months in a rat hole, to come forth for this. He'd go back now and entomb himself forever.

She removed her coat. 'You'd have liked me when I was young, Mitka. I had a sylphlike figure and glorious hair. I was much sought after by men. I was not what you would call sexy but they knew I had it.'

Mitka looked away.

'I had verve and a quality of wholeness. I loved life. In many ways I was too rich for my husband. He couldn't understand my nature and this caused him to leave me – mind you, with two small children.'

She saw he wasn't listening. Olga sighed and burst into tears.

The waiter came.

'One beer. Bring the lady whisky.'

She used two handkerchiefs, one to blow her nose in, the other to dry her eyes.

'You see, Mitka, I told you so.'

Her humility touched him. 'I see.' Why hadn't he, fool, not listened?

She gazed at him with sadly smiling eyes. Without glasses she looked better.

'You're exactly the way I pictured you, except for your thinness which surprises me.'

Olga reached into her market bag and brought out several packages. She unwrapped bread, sausage, herring, Italian cheese, soft salami, pickles and a large turkey drumstick.

'Sometimes I favour myself with these little treats. Eat, Mitka.'

Another landlady. Set Mitka adrift and he enticed some-body's Mama. But he ate, grateful she had provided an oc-cupation.

The waiter brought the drinks. 'What's going on here, a picnic?'

'We're writers,' Olga explained.

'The boss will be pleased.'

'Never mind him, eat, Mitka.'

He ate listlessly. A man had to live. Or did he? When had he felt this low? Probably never.

Olga sipped her whisky. 'Eat, it's self-expression.'

He expressed himself by finishing off the salami, also half the loaf of bread, cheese, and herring. His appetite grew. Searching within the bag Olga brought out a package of sliced corned beef and a ripe pear. He made a sandwich of the meat. On top of that the cold beer was tasty.

'How is the writing going now, Mitka?'

He lowered the glass but changed his mind and gulped the rest.

'Don't speak of it.'

'Be uphearted, not down. Work every day.'

He gnawed the turkey drumstick.

'That's what I do. I've been writing for over twenty years and sometimes – for one reason or another – it gets so bad that I don't feel like going on. But what I do then is relax for a short while and then change to another story. After my juices are flowing again I go back to the other and usually that starts off once more. Or sometimes I discover that it isn't worth bothering over. After you've been writing so long as I you'll learn a system to keep yourself going. It depends on your view of life. If you're mature you'll find out how to work.'

'My writing is a mess,' he sighed, 'a fog, a blot.'

'You'll invent your way out,' said Olga, 'if you only keep trying.'

They sat a while longer. Olga told him of her childhood and when she was a girl. She would have talked longer but Mitka was restless. He was wondering, what after this? Where would he drag that dead cat, his soul?

Olga put what was left of the food into the market bag.

In the street he asked where to.

'The bus I guess. I live on the other side of the river with my son, his vinegary wife and their little daughter.'

He took her bag – a lightened load – and walked with it in one hand, a cigarette in the other, towards the bus terminal.

'I wish you'd known my daughter, Mitka.'

'So why not?' he asked hopefully, surprised he hadn't brought up this before, because she was all the time in the back of his mind.

'She had flowing hair and a sweet hourglass figure. Her nature was beyond compare. You'd have loved her.'

'What's the matter, is she married?'

'She died at twenty – at the fount of life. All my stories are actually about her. Someday I'll collect the best and see if I can get them published.'

He all but crumpled, then walked unsteadily on. For Madeleine he had this night come out of his burrow, to hold her against his lonely heart, but she had burst into fragments, a meteor in reverse, scattered in the far-flung sky, as he stood below, a man mourning.

They came at last to the terminal and Mitka put Olga on the bus.

'Will we meet again, Mitka?'

'Better no,' he said.

'Why not?'

'It makes me sad.'

'Won't you write either? You'll never know what your letters meant to me. I was like a young girl waiting for the mailman.'

'Who knows?' He got off the bus.

She called him to the window. 'Don't worry about your work, and get more fresh air. Build up your body. Good health will help your writing.'

His face showed nothing but he pitied her, her daughter, the world. Why not?

'Character is what counts in the pinches, of course properly mixed with talent. When you saw me in the library and stayed I thought, there is a man of character.'

'Good night,' Mitka said.

'Good night, my dear. Write soon.'

She sat back in her seat and the bus roared out of the depot. As it turned the corner she waved from the window.

Mitka walked the other way. He was momentarily uneasy, until he realized he felt no pangs of hunger. On what he had eaten tonight he could live for a week. Mitka, the camel.

Spring. It gripped and held him. Though he fought the intimacy he was the night's prisoner as he moved towards Mrs Lutz's.

He thought of the old girl. He'd go home now and drape her from head to foot in flowing white. They would jounce together up the stairs, then (strictly a one-marriage man) he would swing her across the threshold, holding her where the fat overflowed her corset as they waltzed around his writing chamber.

Angel Levine

Manischevitz, a tailor, in his fifty-first year suffered many reverses and indignities. Previously a man of comfortable means, he overnight lost all he had, when his establishment caught fire and, after a metal container of cleaning fluid exploded, burned to the ground. Although Manischevitz was insured against fire, damage suits by two customers who had been hurt in the flames deprived him of every penny he had collected. At almost the same time, his son, of much promise, was killed in the war, and his daughter, without so much as a word of warning, married a lout and disappeared with him as off the face of the earth. Thereafter Manischevitz was victimized by excruciating backaches and found himself unable to work even as a presser – the only kind of work available to him – for more than an hour or two daily, because beyond that the pain from standing bècame maddening. His Fanny, a good wife and mother, who had taken in washing and sewing, began before his eyes to waste away. Suffering shortness of breath, she at last became seriously ill and took to her bed. The doctor, a former customer of Manischevitz, who out of pity treated them, at first had difficulty diagnosing her ailment but later put it down as hardening of the arteries at an advanced stage. He took Manischevitz aside, prescribed complete rest for her, and in whispers gave him to know there was little hope.

Throughout his trials Manischevitz had remained somewhat stoic, almost unbelieving that all this had descended upon his head, as if it were happening, let us say, to an acquaintance or some distant relative; it was in sheer quantity of woe incomprehensible. It was also ridiculous, unjust, and because he had always been a religious man, it was in a way an affront to God. Manischevitz believed this in all his suffering. When his burden had grown too crushingly heavy to be borne he prayed in his chair with shut hollow eyes: 'My dear God, sweetheart, did I deserve that this should happen to me?' Then recognizing the worthlessness of it, he put aside the complaint and prayed humbly for assistance: 'Give Fanny back her health, and to me for myself that I shouldn't feel pain in every step. Help now or tomorrow is too late. This I don't have to tell you.' And Manischevitz wept.

Manischevitz's flat, which he had moved into after the disastrous fire, was a meagre one, furnished with a few sticks of chairs, a table, and bed, in one of the poorer sections of the city. There were three rooms: a small, poorly-papered living room; an apology for a kitchen, with a wooden icebox; and the comparatively large bedroom where Fanny lay in a sagging secondhand bed, gasping for breath. The bedroom was the warmest room of the house and it was here, after his outburst to God, that Manischevitz, by the light of two small bulbs overhead, sat reading his Jewish newspaper. He was not truly reading, because his thoughts were everywhere; however the print offered a convenient resting place for his eyes, and a word or two, when he permitted himself to comprehend them, had the momentary effect of helping him forget his troubles. After a short while he discovered, to his surprise, that he was actively scanning the news, searching for an item of great interest to him. Exactly what he thought he would read he couldn't say – until he realized, with some astonishment, that he was expecting to discover something about himself. Manischevitz put his paper down and looked up with the distinct impression that someone had entered the apartment, though he could not remember having heard the sound of the door opening. He looked around: the room was very still, Fanny sleeping, for once, quietly. Half-frightened, he watched her until he was satisfied she wasn't dead; then, still disturbed by the thought of an unannounced visitor, he stumbled into the living room and there had the shock of his life, for at the table sat a Negro reading a newspaper he had folded up to fit into one hand.

'What do you want here?' Manischevitz asked in fright.

The Negro put down the paper and glanced up with a gentle expression. 'Good evening.' He seemed not to be sure of himself, as if he had got into the wrong house. He was a large man, bonily built, with a heavy head covered by a hard derby, which he made no attempt to remove. His eyes seemed sad, but his lips, above which he wore a slight moustache, sought to smile; he was not otherwise prepossessing. The cuffs of his sleeves, Manischevitz noted, were frayed to the lining and the dark suit was badly fitted. He had very large feet. Recovering from his fright, Manischevitz guessed he had left the door open and was being visited by a case worker from the Welfare Department – some came at night – for he had recently applied for relief. Therefore he lowered himself into a chair opposite the Negro, trying, before the man's uncertain smile, to feel comfortable. The former tailor sat stiffly but patiently at the table, waiting for the investigator to take out his pad and pencil and begin asking questions; but before long he became convinced the man intended to do nothing of the sort.

'Who are you?' Manischevitz at last asked uneasily.

'If I may, insofar as one is able to, identify myself, I bear the name of Alexander Levine.'

In spite of all his troubles Manischevitz felt a smile growing on his lips. 'You said Levine?' he politely inquired.

The Negro nodded. 'That is exactly right.'

Carrying the jest farther, Manischevitz asked, 'You are maybe Jewish?'

'All my life I was, willingly.'

The tailor hesitated. He had heard of black Jews but had never met one. It gave an unusual sensation.

Recognizing in afterthought something odd about the tense of Levine's remark, he said doubtfully, 'You ain't Jewish anymore?'

Levine at this point removed his hat, revealing a very white part in his black hair, but quickly replaced it. He replied, 'I have recently been disincarnated into an angel. As such, I offer you my humble assistance, if to offer is within my province and ability – in the best sense.' He lowered his eyes in apology. 'Which calls for added explanation : I am what I am granted to be, and at present the completion is in the future.'

'What kind of angel is this?' Manischevitz gravely asked.

'A bona fide angel of God, within prescribed limitations,' answered Levine, 'not to be confused with the members of any particular sect, order, or organization here on earth operating under a similar name.'

Manischevitz was thoroughly disturbed. He had been expecting something but not this. What sort of mockery was it – provided Levine was an angel – of a faithful servant who had from childhood lived in the synagogues, always concerned with the word of God?

To test Levine he asked, 'Then where are your wings?'

The Negro blushed as well as he was able. Manischevitz understood this from his changed expression. 'Under certain circumstances we lose privileges and prerogatives upon returning to earth, no matter for what purpose, or endeavouring to assist whosoever.'

'So tell me,' Manischevitz said, triumphantly, 'how did you get here?'

'I was transmitted.'

Still troubled, the tailor said, 'If you are a Jew, say the blessing for bread.'

Levine recited it in sonorous Hebrew.

Although moved by the familiar words Manischevitz still felt doubt that he was dealing with an angel.

'If you are an angel,' he demanded somewhat angrily, 'give me the proof.'

Levine wet his lips. 'Frankly, I cannot perform either miracles or near miracles, due to the fact that I am in a condition of probation. How long that will persist or even consist, I admit, depends on the outcome.'

Manischevitz racked his brains for some means of caus-
ing Levine positively to reveal his true identity, when the
Negro spoke again :

'It was given me to understand that both your wife and
you require assistance of a salubrious nature?'

The tailor could not rid himself of the feeling that he was
the butt of a jokester. Is this what a Jewish angel looks like?
he asked himself. This I am not convinced.

He asked a last question. 'So if God sends to me an angel,
why a black? Why not a white that there are so many
of them?'

'It was my turn to go next,' Levine explained.

Manischevitz could not be persuaded. 'I think you are a
faker.'

Levine slowly rose. His eyes showed disappointment and
worry. 'Mr Manischevitz,' he said tonelessly, 'if you should
desire me to be of assistance to you any time in the near
future, or possibly before, I can be found' – he glanced at his
fingernails – 'in Harlem.'

He was by then gone.

The next day Manischevitz felt some relief from his back-
ache and was able to work four hours at pressing. The day
after, he put in six hours; and the third day four again. Fanny
sat up a little and asked for some halvah to suck. But on the
fourth day the stabbing, breaking ache afflicted his back, and
Fanny again lay supine, breathing with blue-lipped difficulty.

Manischevitz was profoundly disappointed at the return of
his active pain and suffering. He had hoped for a longer interval of easement, long enough to have some thought other than
of himself and his troubles. Day by day, hour by hour, minute
after minute, he lived in pain, pain his only memory, ques-
tioning the necessity of it, inveighing against it, also, though
with affection, against God. Why *so much*, Gottenyu? If He
wanted to teach His servant a lesson for some reason, some
cause – the nature of His nature – to teach him, say, for

reasons of his weakness, his pride, perhaps, during his years of prosperity, his frequent neglect of God – to give him a little lesson, why then any of the tragedies that had happened to him, any *one* would have sufficed to chasten him. But *all together* – the loss of both his children, his means of livelihood, Fanny's health and his – that was too much to ask one frail-boned man to endure. Who, after all, was Manischevitz that he had been given so much to suffer? A tailor. Certainly not a man of talent. Upon him suffering was largely wasted. It went nowhere, into nothing: into more suffering. His pain did not earn him bread, nor fill the cracks in the wall, nor lift, in the middle of the night, the kitchen table; only lay upon him, sleepless, so sharply oppressively that he could many times have cried out yet not heard himself through this thickness of misery.

In this mood he gave no thought to Mr Alexander Levine, but at moments when the pain waivered, slightly diminishing, he sometimes wondered if he had been mistaken to dismiss him. A black Jew and angel to boot – very hard to believe, but suppose he *had* been sent to succour him, and he, Manischevitz, was in his blindness too blind to comprehend? It was this thought that put him on the knife-point of agony.

Therefore the tailor, after much self-questioning and continuing doubt, decided he would seek the self-styled angel in Harlem. Of course he had great difficulty, because he had not asked for specific directions, and movement was tedious to him. The subway took him to 116th Street, and from there he wandered in the dark world. It was vast and its lights lit nothing. Everywhere were shadows, often moving. Manischevitz hobbled along with the aid of a cane, and not knowing where to seek in the blackened tenement buildings, looked fruitlessly through store windows. In the stores he saw people and *everybody* was black. It was an amazing thing to observe. When he was too tired, too unhappy to go farther, Manischevitz stopped in front of a tailor's store. Out of familiarity with the appearance of it, with some sadness he entered. The tailor, an old skinny Negro with a mop of woolly grey hair, was sitting cross-legged on his workbench, sewing a pair of full-dress pants that had a razor slit all the way down the seat.

'You'll excuse me, please, gentleman,' said Manischevitz, admiring the tailor's deft, thimbled fingerwork, 'but you know maybe somebody by the name of Alexander Levine?'

The tailor, who Manischevitz thought, seemed a little antagonistic to him, scratched his scalp.

'Cain't say I ever heared dat name.'

'Alex-ander Lev-ine,' Manischevitz repeated it.

The man shook his head. 'Cain't say I heared.'

About to depart, Manischevitz remembered to say: 'He is an angel, maybe.'

'Oh *him*,' said the tailor clucking. 'He hang out in dat honky tonk down here a ways.' He pointed with his skinny finger and returned to the pants.

Manischevitz crossed the street against a red light and was almost run down by a taxi. On the block after the next, the sixth store from the corner was a cabaret, and the name in sparkling lights was Bella's. Ashamed to go in, Manischevitz gazed through the neon-lit window, and when the dancing couples had parted and drifted away, he discovered at a table on the side, towards the rear, Levine.

He was sitting alone, a cigarette butt hanging from the corner of his mouth, playing solitaire with a dirty pack of cards, and Manischevitz felt a touch of pity for him, for Levine had deteriorated in appearance. His derby was dented and had a grey smudge on the side. His ill-fitting suit was shabbier, as if he had been sleeping in it. His shoes and trouser cuffs were muddy, and his face was covered with an impenetrable stubble the colour of liquorice. Manischevitz, though deeply disappointed, was about to enter, when a big-breasted Negress in a purple evening gown appeared before Levine's table, and with much laughter through many white teeth, broke into a vigorous shimmy. Levine looked straight at Manischevitz with a haunted expression, but the tailor was too paralysed to move or acknowledge it. As Bella's gyrations continued, Levine rose, his eyes lit in excitement. She embraced him with vigour, both his hands clasped around her big restless buttocks and they tangoed together across the floor, loudly applauded by the noisy customers. She seemed to have lifted Levine off his feet and his large shoes hung limp as they danced. They slid past the windows where Manischevitz, white-faced, stood staring in. Levine winked slyly and the tailor left for home.

Fanny lay at death's door. Through shrunken lips she muttered concerning her childhood, the sorrows of the marriage bed, the loss of her children, yet wept to live. Manischevitz tried not to listen, but even without ears he would have heard. It was not a gift. The doctor panted up the stairs, a broad but bland, unshaven man (it was Sunday) and soon shook his head. A day at most, or two. He left at once, not without pity, to spare himself Manischevitz's multiplied sorrow; the man who never stopped hurting. He would someday get him into a public home.

Manischevitz visited a synagogue and there spoke to God, but God had absented himself. The tailor searched his heart and found no hope. When she died he would live dead. He considered taking his life although he knew he wouldn't. Yet it was something to consider. Considering, you existed. He railed against God – Can you love a rock, a broom, an emptiness? Baring his chest, he smote the naked bones, cursing himself for having believed.

Asleep in a chair that afternoon, he dreamed of Levine. He was standing before a faded mirror, preening small decaying opalescent wings. 'This means,' mumbled Manischevitz, as he broke out of sleep, 'that it is possible he could be an angel.' Begging a neighbour lady to look in on Fanny and occasionally wet her lips with a few drops of water, he drew on his thin coat, gripped his walking stick, exchanged some pennies for a subway token, and rode to Harlem. He knew this act was the last desperate one of his woe: to go without belief, seeking a black magician to restore his wife to invalidism. Yet if there was no choice, he did at least what was chosen.

He hobbled to Bella's but the place had changed hands. It was now, as he breathed, a synagogue in a store. In the front, towards him, were several rows of empty wooden benches. In the rear stood the Ark, its portals of rough wood covered with rainbows of sequins; under it a long table on which lay the sacred scroll unrolled, illuminated by the dim light from a bulb on a chain overhead. Around the table, as if frozen to it and the scroll which they all touched with their fingers, sat four Negroes wearing skullcaps. Now as they read the Holy Word, Manischevitz could, through the plate glass window, hear the singsong chant of their voices. One of them was old, with a grey beard. One was bubble-eyed. One was hump-backed. The fourth was a boy, no older than thirteen. Their heads moved in rhythmic swaying. Touched by this sight from his childhood and youth, Manischevitz entered and stood silent in the rear.

'Neshoma,' said bubble eyes, pointing to the word with a stubby finger. 'Now what dat mean?'

'That's the word that means soul,' said the boy. He wore glasses.

'Let's git on wid de commentary,' said the old man.

'Ain't necessary,' said the humpback. 'Souls is immaterial substance. That's all. The soul is derived in that manner. The immateriality is derived from the substance, and they both, causally an' otherwise, derived from the soul. There can be no higher.'

'That's the highest.'

'Over de top.'

'Wait a minute,' said bubble eyes. 'I don't see what is dat immaterial substance. How come de one gits hitched up to de odder?' He addressed the humpback.

'Ask me something hard. Because it is substanceless im-materiality. It couldn't be closer together, like all the parts of the body under one skin – closer.'

'Hear now,' said the old man.

'All you done is switched de words.'

'It's the primum mobile, the substanceless substance from

which comes all things that were incepted in the idea – you, me and everything and body else.'

'Now how did all dat happen? Make it sound simple.'

'It de speerit,' said the old man. 'On de face of de water moved de speerit. An' dat was good. It say so in de Book. From de speerit ariz de man.'

'But now listen here. How come it become substance if it all de time a spirit?'

'God alone done dat.'

'Holy! Holy! Praise His Name.'

'But has dis spirit got some kind of a shade or colour?' asked bubble eyes, deadpan.

'Man of course not. A spirit is a spirit.'

'Then how come we is coloured?' he said with a triumphant glare.

'Ain't got nothing to do wid dat.'

'I still like to know.'

'God put the spirit in all things,' answered the boy. 'He put it in the green leaves and the yellow flowers. He put it with the gold in the fishes and the blue in the sky. That's how come it came to us.'

'Amen.'

'Praise Lawd and utter loud His speechless name.'

'Blow de bugle till it bust the sky.'

They fell silent, intent upon the next word. Manischevitz approached them.

'You'll excuse me,' he said. 'I am looking for Alexander Levine. You know him maybe?'

'That's the angel,' said the boy.

'Oh, *him*,' snuffed bubble eyes.

'You'll find him at Bella's. It's the establishment right across the street,' the humpback said.

Manischevitz said he was sorry that he could not stay, thanked them, and limped across the street. It was already night. The city was dark and he could barely find his way.

But Bella's was bursting with the blues. Through the window Manischevitz recognized the dancing crowd and among them sought Levine. He was sitting loose-lipped at Bella's side table. They were tippling from an almost empty whisky fifth. Levine had shed his old clothes, wore a shiny new checkered suit, pearl-grey derby, cigar, and big, two-tone button shoes. To the tailor's dismay, a drunken look had settled upon his formerly dignified face. He leaned towards Bella, tickled her ear lobe with his pinky, while whispering words that sent her into gales of raucous laughter. She fondled his knee.

Manischevitz, girding himself, pushed open the door and was not welcomed.

'This place reserved.'

'Beat it, pale puss.'

'Exit, Yankel, Semitic trash.'

But he moved towards the table where Levine sat, the crowd breaking before him as he hobbled forward.

'Mr Levine,' he spoke in a trembly voice. 'Is here Manischevitz.'

Levine glared blearily. 'Speak yo' piece, son.'

Manischevitz shuddered. His back plagued him. Cold tremors tormented his crooked legs. He looked around, everybody was all ears.

'You'll excuse me. I would like to talk to you in a private place.'

'Speak, Ah is a private pusson.'

Bella laughed piercingly. 'Stop it, boy, you killin' me.'

Manischevitz, no end disturbed, considered fleeing but Levine addressed him:

'Kindly state the pu'pose of yo' communication with yo's truly.'

The tailor wet cracked lips. 'You are Jewish. This I am sure.'

Levine rose, nostrils flaring. 'Anythin' else yo' got to say?'

Manischevitz's tongue lay like stone.

'Speak now or fo'ever hold off.'

Tears blinded the tailor's eyes. Was ever man so tried? Should he say he believed a half-drunken Negro to be an angel?

The silence slowly petrified.

Manischevitz was recalling scenes of his youth as a wheel in his mind whirred: believe, do not, yes, no, yes, no. The pointer pointed to yes, to between yes and no, to no, no it was yes. He sighed. It moved but one had still to make a choice.

'I think you are an angel from God.' He said it in a broken voice, thinking, If you said it it was said. If you believed it you must say it. If you believed, you believed.

The hush broke. Everybody talked but the music began and they went on dancing. Bella, grown bored, picked up the cards and dealt herself a hand.

Levine burst into tears. 'How you have humiliated me.'

Manischevitz apologized.

'Wait'll I freshen up.' Levine went to the men's room and returned in his old clothes.

No one said goodbye as they left.

They rode to the flat via subway. As they walked up the stairs Manischevitz pointed with his cane at his door.

'That's all been taken care of,' Levine said. 'You best go in while I take off.'

Disappointed that it was so soon over but torn by curiosity, Manischevitz followed the angel up three flights to the roof. When he got there the door was already padlocked.

Luckily he could see through a small broken window. He heard an odd noise, as though of a whirring of wings, and when he strained for a wider view, could have sworn he saw a dark figure borne aloft on a pair of magnificent black wings.

A feather drifted down. Manischevitz gasped as it turned white, but it was only snowing.

He rushed downstairs. In the flat Fanny wielded a dust mop under the bed and then upon the cobwebs on the wall.

'A wonderful thing, Fanny,' Manischevitz said. 'Believe me, there are Jews everywhere.'

Behold the Key

One beautiful late-autumn day in Rome, Carl Schneider, a graduate student in Italian studies at Columbia University, left a real estate agent's office after a depressing morning of apartment hunting and walked up Via Veneto, disappointed in finding himself so dissatisfied in this city of his dreams. Rome, a city of perpetual surprise, had surprised unhappily. He felt unpleasantly lonely for the first time since he had been married, and found himself desiring the lovely Italian women he passed in the street, especially the few who looked as if they had money. He had been a damn fool, he thought, to come here with so little of it in his pocket.

He had, last spring, been turned down for a Fulbright fellowship and had had no peace with himself until he decided to go to Rome anyway to do his Ph.D. on the Risorgimento from first-hand sources, at the same time enjoying Italy. This plan had for years aroused his happiest expectations. Norma thought he was crazy to want to take off with two kids under six and all their savings – $3,600, most of it earned by her, but Carl argued that people had to do something different with their lives occasionally or they went to pot. He was twenty-eight – his years weighed on him – and she was thirty, and when else could they go if not now? He was confident, since he knew the language, that they could get settled satisfactorily in a short time. Norma had her doubts. It all came to nothing until her mother, a widow, offered to pay their passage across; then Norma said yes, though still with misgiving.

'We've read prices are terrible in Rome. How do we know we'll get along on what we have?'

'You got to take a chance once in a while,' Carl said.

'Up to a point, with two kids,' Norma replied; but she took the chance and they sailed out of season – the sixteenth of October, arriving in Naples on the twenty-sixth and going on at once to Rome, in the hope they would save money if they found an apartment quickly, though Norma wanted to see Capri and Carl would have liked to spend a little time in Pompeii.

In Rome, though Carl had no trouble getting around or making himself understood, they had immediate rough going trying to locate an inexpensive furnished flat. They had figured on a two-bedroom apartment, Carl to work in theirs; or one bedroom and a large maid's room where the kids would sleep. Although they searched across the city they could locate nothing decent within their means, fifty to fifty-five thousand lire a month, a top of about ninety dollars. Carl turned up some inexpensive places but in hopeless Trastevere sections; elsewhere there was always some other fatal flaw: no heat, missing furniture, sometimes no running water or sanitation.

To make bad worse, during their second week at the dark little pensione where they were staying, the children developed nasty intestinal disorders, little Mike having to be carried to the bathroom ten times one memorable night, and Christine running a temperature of 105; so Norma, who didn't trust the milk or cleanliness of the pensione, suggested they would be better off in a hotel. When Christine's fever abated they moved into the Sora Cecilia, a second-class albergo recommended by a Fulbright fellow they had met. It was a four-storey building full of high-ceilinged, boxlike rooms. The toilets were in the hall, but the rent was comparatively low. About the only other virtue of the place was that it was near the Piazza Navone, a lovely 17th-century square, walled by many magnificently picturesque, wine-coloured houses. Within the piazza three fountains played, whose water and sculpture Carl and Norma enjoyed, but which they soon became insensible to during their sad little walks with the

kids, as the days passed and they still found themselves home-
less.

Carl had in the beginning avoided the real estate agents to
save the commission – 5 per cent of the full year's rent; but
when he gave in and visited their offices they said it was too
late to get anything at the price he wanted to pay.

'You should have come in July,' one agent said.

'I'm here now.'

He threw up his hands. 'I believe in miracles but who can
make them?' Better to pay seventy-five thousand and so live
comfortable like other Americans.

'I can't afford it, not with heat extra.'

'Then you will sit out the winter in the hotel.'

'I appreciate your concern.' Carl left, embittered.

However, they sometimes called him to witness an occasional 'miracle'. One man showed him a pleasant apartment
overlooking some prince or other's formal garden. The rent
was sixty thousand, and Carl would have taken it had he
not later learned from the tenant next door – he had returned
because he distrusted the agent – that the flat was heated
electrically, which would cost twenty thousand a month over
the sixty thousand rent. Another 'miracle' was the offer by
this agent's cousin of a single studio room on the Via
Margutta, for forty thousand. And from time to time a lady
agent called Norma to tell her about this miraculous place
in the Parioli : eight stunning rooms, three bedrooms, double
service, American-style kitchen with refrigerator, garage –
marvellous for an American family : price, two hundred thousand.

'Please, no more,' Norma said.

'I'll go mad,' said Carl. He was nervous over the way time
was flying, almost a month gone, he having given none of it
to his work. And Norma, washing the kids' things in the hotel
sink, in an unheated, cluttered room, was obviously unhappy.
Furthermore, the hotel bill last week had come to twenty
thousand lire, and it was costing them two thousand more
a day to eat badly, even though Norma was cooking the

children's food in their room on a hotplate they had bought.

'Carl, maybe I'd better go to work?'

'I'm tired of your working,' he answered. 'You'll have no fun.'

'What fun am I having? All I've seen is the Colosseum.' She then suggested they could rent an unfurnished flat and build their own furniture.

'Where would I get the tools?' he said. 'And what about the cost of wood in a country where it's cheaper to lay down marble floors? And who'll do my reading for me while I'm building and finishing the stuff?'

'All right,' Norma said. 'Forget I said anything.'

'What about taking a seventy-five thousand place but staying only for five or six months?' Carl said.

'Can you get your research done in five or six months?'

'No.'

'I thought your research was the main reason we came here.' Norma then wished she had never heard of Italy.

'That's enough of that,' said Carl.

He felt helpless, blamed himself for coming – bringing all this on Norma and the kids. He could not understand why things were going so badly. When he was not blaming himself he was blaming the Italians. They were aloof, evasive, indifferent to his plight. He couldn't communicate with them in their own language, whatever it was. He couldn't get them to say what was what, to awaken their hearts to his needs. He felt his plans, his hopes caving in, and feared disenchantment with Italy unless they soon found an apartment.

At the Porta Pinciana, near the tram, Carl felt himself tapped on the shoulder. A bushy-haired Italian, clutching a worn briefcase, was standing in the sun on the sidewalk. His hair rose in all directions. His eyes were gentle; not sad, but they had been. He wore a clean white shirt, rag of a tie, and a black jacket that had crawled a little up his back. His trousers were of denim, and his porous, sharp-pointed shoes, neatly shined, were summer shoes.

'Excuse me,' he said with an uneasy smile. 'I am Vasco Bevilacqua. Weesh you an apotament?'

'How did you guess?' Carl said.

'I follow you,' the Italian answered, making a gesture in the air, 'when you leave the agencia. I am myself agencia. I like to help Americans. They are wonderful people.'

'You're a real estate agent?'

'Eet is just.'

'Parliamo italiano?'

'You spik?' He seemed disappointed. 'Ma non è italiano?'

Carl told him he was an American student of Italian history and culture, had studied the language for years.

Bevilacqua then explained that, although he had no regular office, nor, for that matter, a car, he had managed to collect several exclusive listings. He had got these, he said, from friends who knew he was starting a business, and they made it a habit to inform him of apartments recently vacated in their buildings or those of friends, for which service, he of course tipped them out of his commissions. The regular agents, he went on, demanded a heartless five per cent. He requested only three. He charged less because his expenses, frankly, were low, and also because of his great affection for Americans. He asked Carl how many rooms he was looking for and what he was willing to pay.

Carl hesitated. The man, though pleasant, was no bona fide agent, probably had no licence. He had heard about these two-bit operators and was about to say he wasn't interested but Bevilacqua's eyes pleaded with him not to say it.

Carl figured he had nothing to lose. Maybe he does have a place I might be interested in. He told the Italian what he was looking for and how much he expected to pay.

Bevilacqua's face lit up. 'In weech zone do you seek?' he asked with emotion.

'Any place fairly decent,' Carl said in Italian. 'It doesn't have to be perfect.'

'Not the Parioli?'

'Not the Parioli only. It would depend on the rent.'

Bevilacqua held his briefcase between his knees and fished in his shirt pocket. He drew out a sheet of very thin paper, unfolded it, and read the pencilled writing, with wrinkled brows. After a while he thrust the paper back into his pocket and retrieved his briefcase.

'Let me have your telephone number,' he said in Italian. 'I will examine my other listings and give you a ring.'

'Listen,' Carl said, 'if you've got a good place to show me, all right. If not, please don't waste my time.'

Bevilacqua looked hurt. 'I give you my word,' he said, placing his big hand on his chest, 'tomorrow you will have your apartment. May my mother give birth to a goat if I fail you.'

He put down in a little book where Carl was staying. 'I'll be over at thirteen sharp to show you some miraculous places,' he said.

'Can't you make it in the morning?'

Bevilacqua was apologetic. 'My hours are now from thirteen to sixteen.' He said he hoped to expand his time later, and Carl guessed he was working his real estate venture during his lunch and siesta time, probably from some underpaid clerk's job.

He said he would expect him at thirteen sharp.

Bevilaqua, his expression now so serious he seemed to be listening to it, bowed, and walked away in his funny shoes.

He showed up at the hotel at ten to two, wearing a small black fedora, his hair beaten down with pomade whose odour sprang into the lobby. Carl was waiting restlessly near the desk, doubting he would show up, when Bevilacqua came running through the door, clutching his briefcase.

'Ready?' he said breathlessly.

'Since one o'clock,' Carl answered.

'Ah, that's what comes of not owning your own car,' Bevilacqua explained. 'My bus had a flat tyre.'

Carl looked at him but his face was deadpan. 'Well, let's get on,' the student said.

'I have three places to show you.' Bevilacqua told him the first address, a two-bedroom apartment at just fifty thousand.

On the bus they clung to straps in a tight crowd, the Italian raising himself on his toes and looking around at every stop to see where they were. Twice he asked Carl the time, and when Carl told him, his lips moved soundlessly. After a time Bevilacqua roused himself, smiled, and remarked, 'What do you think of Marilyn Monroe?'

'I haven't much thought of her,' Carl said.

Bevilacqua looked puzzled. 'Don't you go to the movies?'

'Once in a while.'

The Italian made a short speech on the wonder of American films. 'In Italy they always make us look at what we have just lived through.' He fell into silence again. Carl noticed that he was holding in his hand a wooden figurine of a hunchback with a high hat, whose poor gobbo he was rubbing with his thumb, for luck.

'For us both,' Carl hoped. He was still restless, still worried.

But their luck was nil at the first place, an ochre-coloured house behind an iron gate.

'Third floor?' Carl asked, after the unhappy realization that he had been here before.

'Exactly. How did you guess?'

'I've seen the apartment,' he answered gloomily. He remembered having seen an ad. If that was how Bevilacqua got his listings, they might as well quit now.

'But what's wrong with it?' the Italian asked, visibly disappointed.

'Bad heating.'

'How is that possible?'

'They have a single gas heater in the living room but nothing in the bedrooms. They were supposed to have steam heat installed in the building in September, but the contract fell through when the price of steam pipe went up. With two kids, I wouldn't want to spend the winter in a cold flat.'

'Cretins,' muttered Bevilacqua. 'The portiere said the heat was perfect.'

He consulted his paper. 'I have a place in the Prati district, two fine bedrooms and combined living and dining room. Also an American-type refrigerator in the kitchen.'

'Has the apartment been advertised in the papers?'

'Absolutely no. My cousin called me about this one last night – but the rent is fifty-five thousand.'

'Let's see it anyway,' Carl said.

It was an old house, formerly a villa, which had been cut up into apartments. Across the street stood a little park with tall tufted pine trees, just the thing for the kids. Bevilacqua located the portiere, who led them up the stairs, all the while saying how good the flat was. Although Carl discovered at once that there was no hot water in the kitchen sink and it would have to be carried in from the bathroom, the flat made a good impression on him. But then in the master bedroom he noticed that one wall was wet and there was a disagreeable odour in the room.

The portiere quickly explained that a water pipe had burst in the wall, but they would have it fixed in a week.

'It smells like a sewer pipe,' said Carl.

'But they will have it fixed this week,' Bevilacqua said.

'I couldn't live a week with that smell in the room.'

'You mean you are not interested in the apartment?' the Italian said fretfully.

Carl nodded. Bevilacqua's face fell. He blew his nose and they left the house. Outside he regained his calm. 'You can't trust your own mother nowadays. I called the portiere this morning and he guaranteed me the house was without a fault.'

'He must have been kidding you.'

'It makes no difference. I have an exceptional place in mind for you now, but we've got to hurry.'

Carl half-heartedly asked where it was.

The Italian looked embarrassed. 'In the Parioli, a wonderful section, as you know. Your wife won't have to look far for friends – there are Americans all over. Also Japanese and Indians, if you have international tastes.'

'The Parioli,' Carl muttered. 'How much?'

'Only sixty-five thousand,' Bevilacqua said, staring at the ground.

'Only? Still, it must be a dump at that price.'

'It's really very nice – new, and with a good-size nuptial bedroom and one small, besides the usual things, including a fine kitchen. You will personally love the magnificent terrace.'

'Have you seen the place?'

'I spoke to the maid and she says the owner is very anxious to rent. They are moving, for business reasons, to Turin next week. The maid is an old friend of mine. She swears the place is perfect.'

Carl considered it. Sixty-five thousand meant close to a hundred and five dollars. 'Well,' he said after a while, 'let's have a look at it.'

They caught a tram and found seats together, Bevilacqua impatiently glancing out of the window whenever they stopped. On the way he told Carl about his hard life. He was the eighth of twelve children, only five now alive. Nobody was really ever not hungry, though they ate spaghetti by the bucketful. He had to leave school at ten and go to work. In the war he was wounded twice, once by the Americans advancing, and once by the Germans retreating. His father was killed in an allied bombardment of Rome, the same that had cracked open his mother's grave in the Cimitero Verano.

'The British pinpointed their targets,' he said, 'but the Americans dropped bombs everywhere. This was the advantage of your great wealth.'

Carl said he was sorry about the bombardments.

'Nevertheless, I like the Americans better,' Bevilacqua went on. 'They are more like Italians – open. That's why I like to help them when they come here. The British are more closed. They talk with tight lips.' He made sounds with tight lips.

As they were walking towards Piazza Euclide, he asked Carl if he had an American cigarette on him.

'I don't smoke,' Carl said apologetically.

Bevilacqua shrugged and walked faster.

The house he took Carl to was a new one on Via Archimede, an attractive street that wound up and around a hill. It was crowded with long-balconied apartment buildings in bright colours. Carl thought he would be happy to live in one of them. It was a short thought, he wouldn't let it get too long.

They rode up to the fifth floor, and the maid, a dark girl with fuzzy cheeks, showed them through the neat apartment.

'Is sixty-five thousand correct?' Carl asked her.

She said yes.

The flat was so good that Carl, moved by elation and fear, began to pry.

'I told you you'd like it,' Bevilacqua said, rubbing his palms. 'I'll draw up the contract tonight.'

'Let's see the bedroom now,' Carl said.

But first the maid led them onto a broad terrace to show them the view of the city. The sight excited Carl – the variety of architecture from ancient to modern times, where history had been and still, in its own aftermath, sensuously flowed, a sea of roofs, towers, domes; and in the background, golden-domed St Peter's. This marvellous city, Carl thought.

'Now the bedroom,' he said.

'Yes, the bedroom.' The maid led them through double doors into the 'camera matrimoniale,' spacious, and tastefully furnished, containing handsome mahogany twin beds.

'They'll do,' Carl said, to hide his joy, 'though I personally prefer a double bed.'

'I also,' said the maid, 'but you can move one in.'

'These will do.'

'But they won't be here,' she said.

'What do you mean they won't be here?' Bevilacqua demanded.

'Nothing will be left. Everything goes to Turin.'

Carl's beautiful hopes took another long dive into a dirty cellar.

Bevilacqua flung his hat on the floor, landed on it with both feet and punched himself on the head with his fists.

The maid swore she had told him on the phone that the apartment was for rent unfurnished.

He began to yell at her and she shouted at him. Carl left, broken-backed. Bevilacqua caught up with him in the street. It was a quarter to four and he had to rush off to work. He held his hat and ran down the hill.

'I weel show you a terreefic place tomorrow,' he called over his shoulder.

'Over my dead body,' said Carl.

On the way to the hotel he was drenched in a heavy rainfall, the first of many in the late autumn.

The next morning the hotel phone rang at seven-thirty. The children awoke, Mike crying. Carl, dreading the day, groped for the ringing phone. Outside it was still raining.

'Pronto.'

It was a cheery Bevilacqua. 'I call you from my job. I 'ave found for you an apotament een weech you can move to-morrow if you like.'

'Go to hell.'

'Cosa?'

'Why do you call so early? You woke the children.'

'Excuse me,' Bevilacqua said in Italian. 'I wanted to give you the good news.'

'What goddamn good news?'

'I have found a first-class apartment for you near the Monte Sacro. It has only one bedroom but also a combined living and dining room with a double day bed, and a glass-enclosed terrace studio for your studies, and a small maid's room. There is no garage but you have no car. Price forty-five thousand – less than you expected. The apartment is on the ground floor and there is also a garden for your children to play in. Your wife will go crazy when she sees it.'

'So will I,' Carl said. 'Is it furnished?'

Bevilacqua coughed. 'Of course.'

'Of course. Have you been there?'

He cleared his throat. 'Not yet. I just discovered it this minute. The secretary of my office, Mrs Gaspari, told me about it. The apartment is directly under hers. She will make a wonderful neighbour for you. I will come to your hotel precisely at thirteen and a quarter.'

'Give yourself time. Make it fourteen.'

'You will be ready?'

'Yes.'

But when he had hung up, his feeling of dread had grown. He felt afraid to leave the hotel and confessed this to Norma.

'Would you like me to go this time?' she asked.

He considered it but said no.

'Poor Carl.'

' "The great adventure." '

'Don't be bitter. It makes me miserable.'

They had breakfast in the room – tea, bread and jam, fruit. They were cold, but there was to be no heat, it said on a card tacked on the door, until December. Norma put sweaters on the kids. Both had colds. Carl opened a book but could not concentrate and settled for *Il Messaggero*. Norma telephoned the lady agent; she said she would ring back when there was something new to show.

Bevilacqua called up from the lobby at one-forty.

'Coming,' Carl said, his heart heavy.

The Italian was standing in wet shoes near the door. He held his briefcase and a dripping large umbrella but had left his hat home. Even in the damp his bushy hair stood upright. He looked slightly miserable.

They left the hotel. Bevilacqua walking quickly by Carl's side, manoeuvring to keep the umbrella over both of them. On the Piazza Navona a woman was feeding a dozen stray cats in the rain. She had spread a newspaper on the ground and the cats were grabbing hard strings of last night's macaroni. Carl felt the recurrence of his loneliness.

A packet of garbage thrown out of a window hit their umbrella and bounced off. The garbage spilled on the ground. A white-faced man, staring out of a third-floor window, pointed to the cats. Carl shook his fist at him.

Bevilacqua was moodily talking about himself. 'In eight years of hard work I advanced myself only from thirty-thousand lire to fifty-five thousand a month. The cretin who sits on my left in the office has his desk at the door and makes forty thousand extra in tips just to give callers an appointment with the big boss. If I had that desk I would double what he takes in.'

'Have you thought of changing jobs?'

'Certainly, but I could never start at the salary I am now earning. And there are twenty people who will jump into my job at half the pay.'

'Tough,' Carl said.

'For every piece of bread, we have twenty open mouths. You Americans are the lucky ones.'

'Yes, in that way.'

'In what way no?'

'We have no piazzas.'

Bevilacqua shrugged one shoulder. 'Can you blame me for wanting to advance myself?'

'Of course not. I wish you the best.'

'I wish the best to all Americans,' Bevilacqua declared. 'I like to help them.'

'And I to all Italians and pray them to let me live among them for a while.'

'Today it will be arranged. Tomorrow you will move in. I feel luck in my bones. My wife kissed St Peter's toe yesterday.'

Traffic was heavy, a stream of gnats – Vespas, Fiats, Renaults – roared at them from both directions, nobody slowing down to let them pass. They ploughed across dangerously. At the bus stop the crowd rushed for the doors when the bus swerved to the curb. It moved away with its rear door open, four people hanging on the step.

I can do as well in Times Square, Carl thought.

In a half hour, after a short walk from the bus stop, they arrived at a broad, tree-lined street. Bevilacqua pointed to a yellow apartment house on the corner they were approaching. All over it were terraces, the ledges loaded with flower pots and stone boxes dropping ivy over the walls. Carl would not allow himself to think the place had impressed him.

Bevilacqua nervously rang the portiere's bell. He was again rubbing the hunchback's gobbo. A thick-set man in a blue smock came up from the basement. His face was heavy and he wore a full black moustache. Bevilacqua gave him the number of the apartment they wanted to see.

'Ah, there I can't help you,' said the portiere. 'I haven't got the key.'

'Here we go again,' Carl muttered.

'Patience,' Bevilacqua counselled. He spoke to the portiere in a dialect Carl couldn't follow. The portiere made a long speech in the same dialect.

'Come upstairs,' said Bevilacqua.

'Upstairs where?'

'To the lady I told you about, the secretary of my office. She lives on the first floor. We will wait there comfortably until we can get the key to the apartment.'

'Where is it?'

'The portiere isn't sure. He says a certain Contessa owns the apartment but she let her lover live in it. Now the Contessa decided to get married so she asked the lover to move, but he took the key with him.'

'It's that simple,' said Carl.

'The portiere will telephone the Contessa's lawyer who takes care of her affairs. He must have another key. While he makes the call we will wait in Mrs. Gaspari's apartment. She will make you an American coffee. You'll like her husband too, he works for an American company.'

'Never mind the coffee,' Carl said. 'Isn't there some way we can get a look into the flat? For all I know it may not be worth waiting for. Since it's on the ground floor maybe we can have a look through the windows?'

'The windows are covered by shutters which can be raised from the inside only.'

They walked up to the secretary's apartment. She was a dark woman of thirty, with extraordinary legs, and bad teeth when she smiled.

'Is the apartment worth seeing?' Carl asked her.

'It's just like mine, with the exception of having a garden. Would you care to see mine?'

'If I may.'

'Please.'

She led him through her rooms. Bevilacqua remained on the sofa in the living room, his damp briefcase on his knees. He opened the straps, took out a chunk of bread, and chewed thoughtfully.

Carl admitted to himself that he liked the flat. The building was comparatively new, had gone up after the war. The one bedroom was a disadvantage, but the kids could have it and he and Norma would sleep on the day bed in the living room. The terrace studio was perfect for a workroom. He had looked out of the bedroom window and seen the garden, a wonderful place for children to play.

'Is the rent really forty-five thousand?' he asked.

'Exactly.'

'And it is furnished?'

'In quite good taste.'

'Why doesn't the Contessa ask more for it?'

'She has other things on her mind,' Mrs Gaspari laughed. 'Oh, see,' she said, 'the rain has stopped and the sun is coming out. It is a good sign.' She was standing close to him.

'What's in it for her?' Carl thought and then remembered she would share Bevilacqua's poor three per cent.

He felt his lips moving. He tried to stop the prayer but it went on. When he had finished, it began again. The apartment was fine, the garden just the thing for the kids. The price was better than he had hoped.

In the living room Bevilacqua was talking to the portiere. 'He couldn't reach the lawyer,' he said glumly.

'Let me try,' Mrs Gaspari said. The portiere gave her the number and left. She dialled the lawyer but found he had gone for the day. She got his house number and telephoned there. The busy signal came. She waited a minute, then dialled again.

Bevilacqua took two small hard apples from his brief-case and offered one to Carl. Carl shook his head. The Italian peeled the apples with his penknife and ate both. He dropped the skins and cores into his briefcase, then locked the straps.

'Maybe we could take the door down,' Carl suggested. 'It shouldn't be hard to pull the hinges.'

'The hinges are on the inside,' Bevilacqua said.

'I doubt if the Contessa would rent to you,' said Mrs Gaspari from the telephone, 'if you got in by force.'

'If I had the lover here,' Bevilacqua said, 'I would break his neck for stealing the key.'

'Still busy,' said Mrs Gaspari.

'Where does the Contessa live?' Carl asked. 'Maybe I could take a taxi over.'

'I believe she moved recently,' Mrs Gaspari said. 'I once had her address but I have no longer.'

'Would the portiere know it?'

'Possibly.' She called the portiere on the house phone but all he would give her was the Contessa's telephone number. The Contessa wasn't home, her maid said, so they telephoned the lawyer and again got a busy signal. Carl was by now ir-ritated.

Mrs Gaspari called the telephone operator, giving the Con-tessa's number and requesting her home address. The tele-phone operator found the old one but could not locate the new.

'Stupid,' said Mrs Gaspari. Once more she dialled the lawyer.

'I have him,' she announced over the mouthpiece. 'Buon giorno, Avvocato.' Her voice was candy.

Carl heard her ask the lawyer if he had a duplicate key and the lawyer replied for three minutes.

She banged down the phone. 'He has no key. Apparently there is only one.'

'To hell with all this.' Carl got up. 'I'm going back to the United States.'

It was raining again. A sharp crack of thunder split the sky, and Bevilacqua, abandoning his briefcase, rose in fright.

'I'm licked,' Carl said to Norma, the next morning. 'Call the agents and tell them we're ready to pay seventy-five. We've got to get out of this joint.'

'Not before we speak to the Contessa. I'll tell her my troubles and break her heart.'

'You'll get involved and you'll get nowhere,' Carl warned her.

'Please call her anyway.'

'I haven't got her number. I didn't think of asking for it.'

'Find it. You're good at research.'

He considered phoning Mrs Gaspari for the number but remembered she was at work, and he didn't have that number. Recalling the address of the apartment house, he looked it up in the phone book. Then he telephoned the portiere and asked for the Contessa's address and her phone number.

'I'll call you back,' said the portiere, eating as he spoke. 'Give me your telephone.'

'Why bother? Give me her number and save yourself the trouble.'

'I have strict orders from the Contessa never to give her number to strangers. They call up on the phone and annoy her.'

'I'm not a stranger. I want to rent her flat.'

The portiere cleared his throat. 'Where are you staying?'

'Albergo Sora Cecilia.'

'I'll call you back in a quarter of an hour.'

'Have it your way.' He gave the portiere his name.

In forty minutes the phone rang and Carl reached for it. 'Pronto.'

'Signore Schneider?' It was a man's voice – a trifle high.

'Speaking.'

'Permit me,' the man said, in fluent though accented English. 'I am Aldo De Vecchis. It would please me to speak to you in person.'

'Are you a real estate agent?'

'Not precisely, but it refers to the apartment of the Contessa. I am the former occupant.'

'The man with the key?' Carl asked quickly.

'It is I.'

'Where are you now?'

'In the foyer downstairs.'

'Come up, please.'

'Excuse me, but if you will permit, I would prefer to speak to you here.'

'I'll be right down.'

'The lover,' he said to Norma.

'Oh, God.'

He rushed down in the elevator. A thin man in a green suit with cuffless trousers was waiting in the lobby. He was about forty, his face small, his hair wet black, and he wore at a tilt the brownest hat Carl had ever seen. Though his shirt collar was frayed, he looked impeccable. Into the air around him leaked the odour of cologne.

'De Vecchis,' he bowed. His eyes, in a slightly pock-marked face, were restless.

'I'm Carl Schneider. How'd you get my number?'

De Vecchis seemed not to have heard. 'I hope you are enjoying your visit here.'

'I'd enjoy it more if I had a house to live in.'

'Precisely. But what is your impression of Italy?'

'I like the people.'

'There are too many of them.' De Vecchis looked restlessly around. 'Where may we speak? My time is short.'

'Ah,' said Carl. He pointed to a little room where people wrote letters. 'In there.'

They entered and sat at a table, alone in the room.

De Vecchis felt in his pocket for something, perhaps a cigarette, but came up with nothing. 'I won't waste your time,' he said. 'You wish the apartment you saw yesterday? I wish you to have it, it is most desirable. There is also with it a garden of roses. You will love it on a summer night when Rome is hot. However, the practical matter is this. Are you willing to invest a few lire to obtain the privilege of entry?'

'The key?' Carl knew but asked.

'Precisely. To be frank I am not in good straits. To that is added the psychological disadvantage of the aftermath of a love affair with a most difficult woman. I leave you to imagine my present condition. Notwithstanding, the apartment I offer is attractive and the rent, as I understand, is for Americans not too high. Surely this has its value for you?' He attempted a smile but it died in birth.

'I am a graduate student of Italian studies,' Carl said, giving him the facts. 'I've invested all of my savings in this trip abroad to get my Ph.D. dissertation done. I have a wife to support and two children.'

'I hear that your government is most generous to the Fulbright Fellows?'

'You don't understand. I am not a Fulbright Fellow.'

'Whatever it is,' De Vecchis said, drumming his fingertips on the table, 'the price of the key is eighty-thousand lire.'

Carl laughed mirthlessly.

'I beg your pardon?'

Carl rose.

'Is the price too high?'

'It's impossible.'

De Vecchis rubbed his brow nervously. 'Very well, since not all Americans are rich Americans – you see, I am objective – I will reduce the sum by one half. For less than a month's rent the key is yours.'

'Thanks. No dice.'

'Please? I don't understand your expression.'

'I can't afford it. I'd still have a commission to pay the agent.'

'Oh? Then why don't you forget him? I will issue orders to the portiere to allow you to move in immediately. This evening, if you prefer. The Contessa's lawyer will draw up the lease free of charge. And although she is difficult to her lovers, she is an angel to her tenants.'

'I'd like to forget the agent,' Carl said, 'but I can't.'

De Vecchis gnawed his lips. 'I will make it twenty-five thousand,' he said, 'but this is my last and absolute word.'

'No, thanks. I won't be a party to a bribe.'

De Vecchis rose, his small face tight, pale. 'It is people like you who drive us to the hands of the Communists. You try to buy us – our votes, our culture, and then you dare speak of bribes.'

He strode out of the room and through the lobby.

Five minutes later the phone rang. 'Fifteen thousand is my final offer.' His voice was thick.

'Not a cent,' said Carl.

Norma stared at him.

De Vecchis slammed the phone.

The portiere telephoned. He had looked everywhere, he said, but had lost the Contessa's address.

'What about her phone number?' Carl asked.

'It was changed when she moved. The numbers are confused in my mind, the old with the new.'

'Look here,' Carl said, 'I'll tell the Contessa you sent De Vecchis to see me about her apartment.'

'How can you tell her if you don't know her number?' the portiere asked with curiosity. 'It isn't listed in the book.'

'I'll ask Mrs Gaspari for it when she gets home from work, then I'll call the Contessa and tell her what you did.'

'What did I do? Tell me exactly.'

'You sent her former lover, a man she wants to get rid of, to try to squeeze money out of me for something that is none of his business – namely her apartment.'

'Is there no other way than this?' asked the portiere.

'If you tell me her address I will give you one thousand lire.' Carl felt his tongue thicken.

'How shameful,' Norma said from the sink, where she was washing clothes.

'Not more than one thousand?' asked the portiere.

'Not more till I move in.'

The portiere then told him the Contessa's last name and her new address. 'Don't repeat where you got it.'

Carl swore he wouldn't.

He left the hotel on the run, got into a cab, and drove across the Tiber to the Via Cassia, in the country.

The Contessa's maid admitted him into a fabulous place with mosaic floors, gilded furniture, and a marble bust of the Contessa's great-grandfather in the foyer where Carl waited. In twenty minutes the Contessa appeared, a plain-looking woman, past fifty, with dyed blonde hair, black eyebrows, and a short, tight dress. The skin on her arms was wrinkled, but her bosom was enormous and she smelled like a rose garden.

'Please, you must be quick,' she said impatiently. 'There is so much to do. I am preparing for my wedding.'

'Contessa,' said Carl, 'excuse me for rushing in like this, but my wife and I have a desperate need for an apartment and we know that yours on the Via Tirreno is vacant. I'm an American student of Italian life and manners. We've been in Italy almost a month and are still living in a third-rate hotel. My wife is unhappy. The children have miserable colds. I'll be glad to pay you fifty-thousand lire, instead of the forty-five you ask, if you will kindly let us move in today.'

'Listen,' said the Contessa, 'I come from an honourable family. Don't try to bribe me.'

Carl blushed. 'I mean nothing more than to give you proof of my good will.'

'In any case, my lawyer attends to my real estate matters.'

'He hasn't the key.'

'Why hasn't he?'

'The former occupant took it with him.'

'The fool,' she said.

'Do you happen to have a duplicate?'

'I never keep duplicate keys. They all get mixed up and I never know which is which.'

'Could we have one made?'

'Ask my lawyer.'

'I called this morning but he's out of town. May I make a suggestion, Contessa? Could we have a window or a door forced? I will pay the cost of repair.'

The Contessa's eyes glinted. 'Of course not,' she said huffily. 'I will have no destruction of my property. We've had enough of that sort of thing here. You Americans have no idea what we've lived through.'

'But doesn't it mean something to you to have a reliable tenant in your apartment? What good is it standing empty? Say the word and I'll bring you the rent in an hour.'

'Come back in two weeks, young man, after I finish my honeymoon.'

'In two weeks I may be dead,' Carl said.

The Contessa laughed.

Outside, he met Bevilacqua. He had a black eye and a stricken expression.

'So you've betrayed me?' the Italian said hoarsely.

'What do you mean "betrayed"? Who are you, Jesus Christ?'

'I hear you went to De Vecchis and begged for the key, with plans to move in without telling me.'

'How could I keep that a secret with your pal Mrs Gaspari living right over my head? The minute I moved in she'd tell you, then you'd be over on horseback to collect.'

'That's right,' said Bevilacqua. 'I didn't think of it.'

'Who gave you the black eye?' Carl asked.

'De Vecchis. He's as strong as a wild pig. I met him at the

apartment and asked for the key. He called me dirty names. We had a fight and he hit me in the eye with his elbow. How did you make out with the Contessa?'

'Not well. Did you come to see her?'

'Vaguely.'

'Go in and beg her to let me move in, for God's sake. Maybe she'll listen to a countryman.'

'Don't ask me to eat a horse,' said Bevilacqua.

That night Carl dreamed they had moved out of the hotel into the Contessa's apartment. The children were in the garden, playing among the roses. In the morning he decided to go to the portiere and offer him ten thousand lire if he would have a new key made, however they did it – door up or door down.

When he arrived at the apartment house the portiere and Bevilacqua were there with a toothless man, on his knees, poking a hooked wire into the door lock. In two minutes it clicked open.

With a gasp they all entered. From room to room they wandered like dead men. The place was a ruin. The furniture had been smashed with a dull axe. The slashed sofa revealed its inner springs. Rugs were cut up, crockery broken, books wildly torn and scattered. The white walls had been splashed with red wine, except one in the living room which was decorated with dirty words in six languages, printed in orange lipstick.

'Mamma mia,' muttered the toothless locksmith, crossing himself. The portiere slowly turned yellow. Bevilacqua wept.

De Vecchis, in his pea green suit, appeared in the doorway. 'Ecco la chiave!' He held it triumphantly aloft.

'Assassin!' shouted Bevilacqua. 'Turd! May your bones grow hair and rot.'

'He lives for my death,' he cried to Carl, 'I for his. This is our condition.'

'You lie,' said Carl. 'I love this country.'

De Vecchis flung the key at them and ran. Bevilacqua, the light of hatred in his eyes, ducked, and the key hit Carl on the forehead, leaving a mark he could not rub out.

Take Pity

Davidov, the census-taker, opened the door without knocking, limped into the room and sat wearily down. Out came his notebook and he was on the job. Rosen, the ex-coffee salesman, wasted, eyes despairing, sat motionless, cross-legged, on his cot. The square, clean but cold room, lit by a dim globe, was sparsely furnished: the cot, a folding chair, small table, old unpainted chests – no closets but who needed them? – and a small sink with a rough piece of green, institutional soap on its holder – you could smell it across the room. The worn black shade over the single narrow window was drawn to the ledge, surprising Davidov.

'What's the matter you don't pull the shade up?' he remarked.

Rosen ultimately sighed. 'Let it stay.'

'Why? Outside is light.'

'Who needs light?'

'What then you need?'

'Light I don't need,' replied Rosen.

Davidov, sour-faced, flipped through the closely scrawled pages of his notebook until he found a clean one. He attempted to scratch in a word with his fountain pen but it had run dry, so he fished a pencil stub out of his vest pocket and sharpened it with a cracked razor blade. Rosen paid no attention to the feathery shavings falling to the floor. He looked restless, seemed to be listening to or for something, although Davidov was convinced there was absolutely nothing to listen to. It was only when the census-taker somewhat irritably and with increasing loudness repeated a question, that Rosen stirred and identified himself. He was about to furnish an address but caught himself and shrugged.

Davidov did not comment on the salesman's gesture. 'So begin,' he nodded.

'Who knows where to begin?' Rosen stared at the drawn shade. 'Do they know here where to begin?'

'Philosophy we are not interested,' said Davidov. 'Start in how you met her.'

'Who?' pretended Rosen.

'Her,' he snapped.

'So if I got to begin, how you know about her already?' Rosen asked triumphantly.

Davidov spoke wearily, 'You mentioned before.'

Rosen remembered. They had questioned him upon his arrival and he now recalled blurting out her name. It was perhaps something in the air. It did not permit you to retain what you remembered. That was part of the cure, if you wanted a cure.

'Where I met her –?' Rosen murmured. 'I met her where she always was – in the back room there in that hole in the wall that it was a waste of time for me I went there. Maybe I sold them a half a bag of coffee a month. This is not business.'

'In business we are not interested.'

'What then you are interested?' Rosen mimicked Davidov's tone.

Davidov clammed up coldly.

Rosen knew they had him where it hurt, so he went on: 'The husband was maybe forty, Axel Kalish, a Polish refugee. He worked like a blind horse when he got to America, and saved maybe two – three thousand dollars that he bought with the money this pisher grocery in a dead neighbourhood where he didn't have a chance. He called my company up for credit and they sent me I should see. I recommended okay because I felt sorry. He had a wife, Eva, you know already about her, and two darling girls, one five and one three, little dolls, Fega and Surale, that I didn't want them to suffer. So right away I told him, without tricks, "Kiddo, this is a mistake. This place is a grave. Here they will bury you if you don't get out quick !" '

Rosen sighed deeply.

'So?' Davidov had thus far written nothing, irking the ex-salesman.

'So? – Nothing. He didn't get out. After a couple months he tried to sell but nobody bought, so he stayed and starved. They never made expenses. Every day they got poorer you couldn't look in their faces. "Don't be a damn fool," I told him, "go in bankruptcy." But he couldn't stand it to lose all his capital, and he was also afraid it would be hard to find a job. "My God," I said, "do anything. Be a painter, a janitor, a junk man, but get out of here before everybody is a skeleton."

'This he finally agreed with me, but before he could go in auction he dropped dead.'

Davidov made a note. 'How did he die?'

'On this I am not an expert,' Rosen replied. 'You know better than me.'

'How did he die?' Davidov spoke impatiently. 'Say in one word.'

'From what he died? – he died, that's all.'

'Answer, please, this question.'

'Broke in him something. That's how.'

'Broke what?'

'Broke what breaks. He was talking to me how bitter was his life, and he touched me on my sleeve to say something else, but the next minute his face got small and he fell down dead, the wife screaming, the little girls crying that it made in my heart pain. I am myself a sick man and when I saw him laying on the floor, I said to myself, "Rosen, say goodbye, this guy is finished." So I said it.'

Rosen got up from the cot and strayed despondently around the room, avoiding the window. Davidov was occupying the only chair, so the ex-salesman was finally forced to sit on the edge of the bed again. This irritated him. He badly wanted a cigarette but disliked asking for one.

Davidov permitted him a short interval of silence, then

leafed impatiently through his notebook. Rosen, to needle the census-taker, said nothing.

'So what happened?' Davidov finally demanded.

Rosen spoke with ashes in his mouth. 'After the funeral –' he paused, tried to wet his lips, then went on, 'He belonged to a society that they buried him, and he also left a thousand dollars insurance, but after the funeral I said to her, "Eva, listen to me. Take the money and your children and run away from here. Let the creditors take the store. What will they get? – Nothing."

'But she answered me, "Where will I go, where, with my two orphans that their father left them to starve?"

' "Go anywhere," I said. "Go to your relatives."

'She laughed like laughs somebody who hasn't got no joy. "My relatives Hitler took away from me."

' "What about Axel – surely an uncle somewheres?"

' "Nobody," she said. "I will stay here like my Axel wanted. With the insurance I will buy new stock and fix up the store. Every week I will decorate the window, and in this way gradually will come in new customers –"

' "Eva, my darling girl –"

' "A millionaire I don't expect to be. All I want is I should make a little living and take care on my girls. We will live in the back here like before, and in this way I can work and watch them, too."

' "Eva," I said, "you are a nice-looking young woman, only thirty-eight years. Don't throw away your life here. Don't flush in the toilet – you should excuse me – the thousand poor dollars from your dead husband. Believe me, I know from such stores. After thirty-five years' experience I know a grave-yard when I smell it. Go better some place and find a job. You're young yet. Sometime you will meet somebody and get married."

' "No, Rosen, not me," she said. "With marriage I am finished. Nobody wants a poor widow with two children."

' "This I don't believe it."

' "I know," she said.

'Never in my life I saw so bitter a woman's face.

' "No," I said. "No."

' "Yes, Rosen, yes. In my whole life I never had anything. In my whole life I always suffered. I don't expect better. This is my life." '

'I said no and she said yes. What could I do? I am a man with only one kidney, and worse than that, that I won't mention it. When I talked she didn't listen, so I stopped to talk. Who can argue with a widow?'

The ex-salesman glanced up at Davidov but the census-taker did not reply. 'What happened then?' he asked.

'What happened?' mocked Rosen. 'Happened what happens.'

Davidov's face grew red.

'What happened, happened,' Rosen said hastily. 'She ordered from the wholesalers all kinds goods that she paid for them cash. All week she opened boxes and packed on the shelves cans, jars, packages. Also she cleaned, and she washed, and she mopped with oil the floor. With tissue paper she made new decorations in the window, everything should look nice – but who came in? Nobody except a few poor customers from the tenement around the corner. And when they came? When was closed the supermarkets and they needed some little item that they forgot to buy, like a quart milk, fifteen cents' cheese, a small can sardines for lunch. In a few months was again dusty the cans on the shelves, and her thousand was gone. Credit she couldn't get except from me, and from me she got because I paid out of my pocket the company. This she didn't know. She worked, she dressed clean, she waited that the store should get better. Little by little the shelves got empty, but where was the profit? They ate it up. When I looked on the little girls I knew what she didn't tell me. Their faces were white, they were thin, they were hungry. She kept the little food that was left, on the shelves. One night I brought in a nice piece sirloin, but I could see from her eyes that she didn't like that I did it. So what else could I do? I have a heart and I am human.'

Here the ex-salesman wept.

Davidov pretended not to see though once he peeked.

Rosen blew his nose, then went on more calmly, 'When the children were sleeping we sat in the dark there, in the back, and not once in four hours opened the door should come in a customer. "Eva, for Godsakes, *run away*," I said.

' "I have no place to go," she said.

' "I will give you where you can go, and please don't say to me no. I am a bachelor, this you know. I got whatever I need and more besides. Let me help you and the children. Money don't interest me. Interests me good health, but I can't buy it. I'll tell you what I will do. Let this place go to the creditors and move into a two-family house that I own, which the top floor is now empty. Rent will cost you nothing. In the meantime you can go and find a job. I will also pay the downstairs lady to take care of the girls – God bless them – until you will come home. With your wages you will buy the food, if you need clothes, and also save a little. This you can use when you get married someday. What do you say?"

'She didn't answer me. She only looked on me in such a way, with such burning eyes, like I was small and ugly. For the first time I thought to myself, "Rosen, this woman don't like you."

' "Thank you very kindly, my friend Mr Rosen," she answered me, "but charity we are not needing. I got yet a paying business, and it will get better when times are better. Now is bad times. When comes again good times will get better the business."

' "Who charity?" I cried to her. "What charity? Speaks to you your husband's a friend."

' "Mr Rosen, my husband didn't have no friends."

' "Can't you see that I want to help the children?"

' "The children have their mother."

' "Eva, what's the matter with you?" I said. "Why do you make sound bad something that I mean it should be good?"

'This she didn't answer. I felt sick in my stomach, and was coming also a headache so I left.

'All night I didn't sleep, and then all of a sudden I figured

out a reason why she was worried. She was worried I would
ask for some kind payment except cash. She got the wrong
man. Anyway, this made me think of something that I didn't
think about before. I thought now to ask her to marry me.
What did she have to lose? I could take care of myself without
any trouble to them. Fega and Surale would have a father he
could give them for the movies, or sometime to buy a little doll
to play with, and when I died, would go to them my investments and insurance policies.

'The next day I spoke to her.

' "For myself, Eva, I don't want a thing. Absolutely not a
thing. For you and your girls – everything. I am not a strong
man, Eva. In fact, I am sick. I tell you this you should understand I don't expect to live long. But even for a few years
would be nice to have a little family."

'She was with her back to me and didn't speak.

'When she turned around again her face was white but the
mouth was like iron.

' "No, Mr Rosen."

' "Why not, tell me?"

' "I had enough with sick men." She began to cry. "Please,
Mr Rosen. Go home."

'I didn't have strength I should argue with her, so I went
home. I went home but hurt me my mind. All day long and all
night I felt bad. My back pained me where was missing my
kidney. Also too much smoking. I tried to understand this
woman but I couldn't. Why should somebody that her two
children were starving always say no to a man that he wanted
to help her? What did I do to her bad? Am I maybe a mur-
derer she should hate me so much? All that I felt in my heart
was pity for her and the children, but I couldn't convince her.
Then I went back and begged her she should let me help them,
and once more she told me no.

' "Eva," I said, "I don't blame you that you don't want a
sick man. So come with me to a marriage broker and we will
find you a strong, healthy husband that he will support you
and your girls. I will give the dowry."

'She screamed, "On this I don't need your help, Rosen!"'

'I didn't say no more. What more could I say? All day long, from early in the morning till late in the night she worked like an animal. All day she mopped, she washed with soap and a brush the shelves, the few cans she polished, but the store was still rotten. The little girls I was afraid to look at. I could see in their faces their bones. They were tired, they were weak. Little Surale held with her hand all the time the dress of Fega. Once when I saw them in the street I gave them some cakes, but when I tried the next day to give them something else, the mother shouldn't know, Fega answered me, "We can't take, Momma says today is a fast day."'

'I went inside. I made my voice soft. "Eva, on my bended knee, I am a man with nothing in this world. Allow me that I should have a little pleasure before I die. Allow me that I should help you to stock up once more the store."'

'So what did she do? She cried, it was terrible to see. And after she cried, what did she say? She told me to go away and I shouldn't come back. I felt like to pick up a chair and break her head.'

'In my house I was too weak to eat. For two days I took in my mouth nothing except maybe a spoon of chicken noodle soup, or maybe a glass tea without sugar. This wasn't good for me. My health felt bad.'

'Then I made up a scheme that I was a friend of Axel's who lived in Jersey. I said I owed Axel seven hundred dollars that he lent me this money fifteen years ago, before he got married. I said I did not have the whole money now, but I would send her every week twenty dollars till it was paid up the debt. I put inside the letter two tens and gave it to a friend of mine, also a salesman, he should mail it in Newark so she would not be suspicious who wrote the letters.'

To Rosen's surprise Davidov had stopped writing. The book was full, so he tossed it onto the table, yawned, but listened amiably. His curiosity had died.

Rosen got up and fingered the notebook. He tried to read

the small distorted handwriting but could not make out a single word.

'It's not English and it's not Yiddish,' he said. 'Could it be in Hebrew?'

'No,' answered Davidov. 'It's an old-fashioned language that they don't use it nowadays.'

'Oh?' Rosen returned to the cot. He saw no purpose to going on now that it was not required, but he felt he had to.

'Came back all the letters,' he said dully. 'The first she opened it, then pasted back again the envelope, but the rest she didn't even open.'

' "Here," I said to myself, "is a very strange thing – a person that you can never give her anything. – But I will give."

'I went then to my lawyer and we made out a will that everything I had – all my investments, my two houses that I owned, also furniture, my car, the checking account – every cent would go to her, and when she died, the rest would be left for the two girls. The same with my insurance. They would be my beneficiaries. Then I signed and went home. In the kitchen I turned on the gas and put my head in the stove.

'Let her say now no.'

Davidov, scratching his stubbled cheek, nodded. This was the part he already knew. He got up and before Rosen could cry no, idly raised the window shade.

It was twilight in space but a woman stood before the window.

Rosen with a bound was off his cot to see.

It was Eva, staring at him with haunted, beseeching eyes. She raised her arms to him.

Infuriated, the ex-saleman shook his fist.

'Whore, bastard, bitch,' he shouted at her. 'Go 'way from here. Go home to your children.'

Davidov made no move to hinder him as Rosen rammed down the window shade.

The Prison

Though he tried not to think of it, at twenty-nine Tommy Castelli's life was a screaming bore. It wasn't just Rosa or the store they tended for profits counted in pennies, or the unendurably slow hours and endless drivel that went with selling candy, cigarettes, and soda water; it was this sick-in-the-stomach feeling of being trapped in old mistakes, even some he had made before Rosa changed Tony into Tommy. He had been as Tony a kid of many dreams and schemes, especially getting out of this tenement-crowded, kid-squawking neighbourhood, with its lousy poverty, but everything had fouled up against him before he could. When he was sixteen he quite the vocational school where they were making him into a shoemaker, and began to hang out with the grey-hatted, thick-soled-shoe boys, who had the spare time and the mazuma and showed it in fat wonderful rolls down in the cellar clubs to all who would look, and everybody did, popeyed. They were the ones who had bought the silver caffe espresso urn and later the television, and they arranged the pizza parties and had the girls down; but it was getting in with them and their cars, leading to the holdup of a liquor store, that had started all the present trouble. Lucky for him the coal-and-ice man who was their landlord knew the leader in the district, and they arranged something so nobody bothered him after that. Then before he knew what was going on – he had been frightened sick by the whole mess – there was his father cooking up a deal with Rosa Agnello's old man that Tony would marry her and the father-in-law would, out of his savings, open a candy store for him to make an honest living. He wouldn't spit on a candy store, and Rosa was too plain and lank a chick for his personal taste, so he beat it off to Texas and bummed around in too much space, and when he came back everybody said it was for Rosa and the candy store, and it was all arranged again and he, without saying no, was in it.

That was how he had landed on Prince Street in the Village, working from eight in the morning to almost midnight every day, except for an hour off each afternoon when he went upstairs to sleep, and on Tuesdays, when the store was closed and he slept some more and went at night alone to the movies. He was too tired always for schemes now, but once he tried to make a little cash on the side by secretly taking in punchboards some syndicate was distributing in the neighbourhood, on which he collected a nice cut and in this way saved fifty-five bucks that Rosa didn't know about; but then the syndicate was written up by a newspaper, and the punchboards all disappeared. Another time, when Rosa was at her mother's house, he took a chance and let them put in a slot machine that could guarantee a nice piece of change if he kept it long enough. He knew of course he couldn't hide it from her, so when she came and screamed when she saw it, he was ready and patient, for once not yelling back when she yelled, and he explained it was not the same as gambling because anybody who played it got a roll of mints every time he put in a nickel. Also the machine would supply them a few extra dollars cash they could use to buy television so he could see the fights without going to a bar; but Rosa wouldn't let up screaming, and later her father came in shouting that he was a criminal and chopped the machine apart with a plumber's hammer. The next day the cops raided for slot machines and gave out summonses wherever they found them, and though Tommy's place was practically the only candy store in the neighbourhood that didn't have one, he felt bad about the machine for a long time.

Mornings had been his best time of day because Rosa stayed upstairs cleaning, and since few people came into the store till noon, he could sit around alone, a toothpick in his teeth, looking over the *News* and *Mirror* on the fountain counter, or maybe gab with one of the old cellar-club guys who had happened to come by for a pack of butts, about a horse that was running that day or how the numbers were paying lately; or just sit there, drinking coffee and thinking how far away he could get on the fifty-five he had stashed away in the cellar. Generally the mornings were this way, but after the slot machine, usually the whole day stank and he along with it. Time rotted in him, and all he could think of the whole morning, was going to sleep in the afternoon, and he would wake up with the sour remembrance of the long night in the store ahead of him, while everybody else was doing as he damn pleased. He cursed the candy store and Rosa, and cursed, from its beginning, his unhappy life.

It was on one of these bad mornings that a ten-year-old girl from around the block came in and asked for two rolls of coloured tissue paper, one red and one yellow. He wanted to tell her to go to hell and stop bothering, but instead went with bad grace to the rear, where Rosa, whose bright idea it was to keep the stuff, had put it. He went from force of habit, for the girl had been coming in every Monday since the summer for the same thing, because her rock-faced mother, who looked as if she arranged her own widowhood, took care of some small kids after school and gave them the paper to cut out dolls and such things. The girl, whose name he didn't know, resembled her mother, except her features were not quite so sharp and she had very light skin with dark eyes; but she was a plain kid and would be more so at twenty. He had noticed, when he went to get the paper, that she always hung back as if afraid to go where it was dark, though he kept the comics there and most of the other kids had to be slapped away from them; and that when he brought her the tissue paper her skin seemed to grow whiter and her eyes shone. She always handed him two hot dimes and went out without glancing back.

It happened that Rosa, who trusted nobody, had just hung a mirror on the back wall, and as Tommy opened the drawer to get the girl her paper this Monday morning that he felt so bad, he looked up and saw in the glass something that made it seem as if he were dreaming. The girl had disappeared, but he saw a white hand reach into the candy case for a chocolate bar and for another, then she came forth from behind the counter and stood there, innocently waiting for him. He felt at first like grabbing her by the neck and socking till she threw up, but he had been caught, as he sometimes was, by this thought of how his Uncle Dom, years ago before he went away, used to take with him Tony alone of all the kids, when he went crabbing to Sheepshead Bay. Once they went at night and threw the baited wire traps into the water and after a while pulled them up and they had this green lobster in one, and just then this fat-faced cop came along and said they had to throw it back unless it was nine inches. Dom said it was nine inches, but the cop said not to be a wise guy so Dom measured it and it was ten, and they laughed about that lobster all night. Then he remembered how he had felt after Dom was gone, and tears filled his eyes. He found himself thinking about the way his life had turned out, and then about this girl, moved that she was so young and a thief. He felt he ought to do something for her, warn her to cut it out before she got trapped and fouled up her life before it got started. His urge to do this was strong, but when he went forward she looked up frightened because he had taken so long. The fear in her eyes bothered him and he didn't say anything. She thrust out the dimes, grabbed at the tissue rolls and ran out of the store.

He had to sit down. He kept trying to make the desire to speak to her go away but it came back stronger than ever. He asked himself what difference does it make if she swipes candy – so she swipes it; and the role of reformer was strange and distasteful to him, yet he could not convince himself that what he felt he must do was unimportant. But he worried he would not know what to say to her. Always he had trouble speaking right, stumbled over words, especially in new situations. He was afraid he would sound like a jerk and she would not take him seriously. He had to tell her in a sure way so that even if it scared her, she would understand he had done it to set her straight. He mentioned her to no one but often thought about her, always looking around whenever he went outside to raise the awning or wash the window, to see if any of the girls playing in the street was her, but they never were. The following Monday, an hour after opening the store he had smoked a full pack of butts. He thought he had found what he wanted to say but was afraid for some reason she wouldn't come in, or if she did, this time she would be afraid to take the candy. He wasn't sure he wanted that to happen until he had said what he had to say. But at about eleven, while he was reading the News, she appeared, asking for the tissue paper, her eyes shining so he had to look away. He knew she meant to steal. Going to the rear he slowly opened the drawer, keeping his head lowered as he sneaked a look into the glass and saw her slide behind the counter. His heart beat hard and his feet felt nailed to the floor. He tried to remember what he had intended to do, but his mind was like a dark, empty room so he let her, in the end, slip away and stood tongue-tied, the dimes burning his palm.

Afterwards, he told himself that he hadn't spoken to her because it was while she still had the candy bar on her, and she would have been scared worse than he wanted. When he went upstairs, instead of sleeping, he sat at the kitchen window, looking out into the back yard. He blamed himself for being too soft, too chicken, but then he thought, no there was a better way to do it. He would do it indirectly, slip her a hint he knew, and he was pretty sure that would stop her. Sometime after, he would explain her why it was good she had stopped. So next time he cleaned out this candy platter she helped herself from, thinking she might get wise he was on to her, but she seemed not to, only hesitated with her hand before she took two candy bars from the next plate and dropped them into the black patent leather purse she always had with her. The time after that he cleaned out the whole top shelf, and still she was not suspicious, and reached down to the next and took something different. One Monday he put some loose change, nickels and dimes, on the candy plate, but she left them there, only taking the candy, which bothered him a little. Rosa asked him what he was mooning about so much and why was he eating chocolate lately. He didn't answer her, and she began to look suspiciously at the women who came in, not excluding the little girls; and he would have been glad to rap her in the teeth, but it didn't matter as long as she didn't know what he had on his mind. At the same time he figured he would have to do something sure soon, or it would get harder for the girl to stop her stealing. He had to be strong about it. Then he thought of a plan that satisfied him. He would leave two bars on the plate and put in the wrapper of one a note she could read when she was alone. He tried out on paper many messages to her, and the one that seemed best he cleanly printed on a strip of cardboard and slipped it under the wrapper of one chocolate bar. It said, 'Don't do this any more or you will suffer your whole life.' He puzzled whether to sign it A Friend or Your Friend and finally chose Your Friend.

This was Friday, and he could not hold his impatience for Monday. But on Monday she did not appear. He waited for a long time, until Rosa came down, then he had to go up and the girl still hadn't come. He was greatly disappointed because she had never failed to come before. He lay on the bed, his shoes on, staring at the ceiling. He felt hurt, the sucker she had played him for and was now finished with because she probably had another on her hook. The more he thought about it the worse he felt. He worked up a splitting headache that kept him from sleeping, then he suddenly slept and woke without it. But he had awaked depressed, saddened. He thought about Dom getting out of jail and going away God knows where. He wondered whether he would ever meet up with him somewhere, if he took the fifty-five bucks and left. Then he remembered Dom was a pretty old guy now, and he might not know him if they did meet. He thought about life. You never really got what you wanted. No matter how hard you tried you made mistakes and couldn't get past them. You could never see the sky outside or the ocean because you were in a prison, except nobody called it a prison, and if you did they didn't know what you were talking about, or they said they didn't. A pall settled on him. He lay motionless, without thought or sympathy for himself or anybody.

But when he finally went downstairs, ironically amused that Rosa had allowed him so long a time off without bitching, there were people in the store and he could hear her screeching. Shoving his way through the crowd he saw in one sickening look that she had caught the girl with the candy bars and was shaking her so hard the kid's head bounced back and forth like a balloon on a stick. With a curse he tore her away from the girl, whose sickly face showed the depth of her fright.

'Whatsamatter,' he shouted at Rosa, 'you want her blood?'

'She's a thief,' cried Rosa.

'Shut your face.'

To stop her yowling he slapped her across her mouth, but it was a harder crack than he had intended. Rosa fell back with a gasp. She did not cry but looked around dazedly at everybody, and tried to smile, and everybody there could see her teeth were flecked with blood.

'Go home,' Tommy ordered the girl, but then there was a movement near the door and her mother came into the store.

'What happened?' she said.

'She stole my candy,' Rosa cried.

'I let her take it,' said Tommy.

Rosa stared at him as if she had been hit again, then with mouth distorted began to sob.

'One was for you, Mother,' said the girl.

Her mother socked her hard across the face. 'You little thief, this time you'll get your hands burned good.'

She pawed at the girl, grabbed her arm and yanked it. The girl, like a grotesque dancer, half ran, half fell forward, but at the door she managed to turn her white face and thrust out at him her red tongue.

The Lady of the Lake

Henry Levin, an ambitious, handsome thirty, who walked the floors in Macy's book department wearing a white flower in his lapel, having recently come into a small inheritance, quit, and went abroad seeking romance. In Paris, for no reason he was sure of, except that he was tired of the past – tired of the limitations it had imposed upon him; although he had signed the hotel register with his right name, Levin took to calling himself Henry R. Freeman. Freeman lived for a short while in a little hotel on a narrow gas lamp-lit street near the Luxembourg Gardens. In the beginning he liked the sense of foreignness of the city – of things different, anything likely to happen. He liked, he said to himself, the possible combinations. But not much did happen; he met no one he particularly cared for (he had sometimes in the past deceived himself about women, they had come to less than he had expected); and since the heat was hot and tourists underfoot, he felt he must flee. He boarded the Milan express, and after Dijon, developed a painful, palpitating anxiety. This grew so troublesome that he had serious visions of leaping off the train, but reason prevailed and he rode on. However, he did not get to Milan. Nearing Stresa, after a quick, astonished look at Lake Maggiore, Freeman, a nature lover from early childhood, pulled his suitcase off the rack and hurriedly left the train. He at once felt better.

An hour later he was established in a pensione in a villa not far from the line of assorted hotels fronting the Stresa shore. The padrona, a talkative woman, much interested in her guests, complained that June and July had been lost in unseasonable cold and wet. Many had cancelled; there were few

Americans around. This didn't exactly disturb Freeman, who had had his full share of Coney Island. He lived in an airy, French-windowed room, including soft bed and spacious bath, and though personally the shower type, was glad of the change. He was very fond of the balcony at his window, where he loved to read, or study Italian, glancing up often to gaze at the water. The long blue lake, sometimes green, sometimes gold, went out of sight among distant mountains. He liked the red-roofed town of Pallanza on the opposite shore, and especially the four beautiful islands in the water, tiny but teeming with palazzi, tall trees, gardens, visible statuary. The sight of these islands aroused in Freeman a deep emotion; each a universe – how often do we come across one in a lifetime? – filled him with expectancy. Of what, he wasn't sure. Freeman still hoped for what he hadn't, what few got in the world and many dared not think of; to wit, love, adventure, freedom. Alas, the words by now sounded slightly comical. Yet there were times, when he was staring at the islands, if you pushed him a little he could almost cry. Ah, what names of beauty: Isola Bella, dei Pescatori, Madre, and del Dongo. Travel is truly broadening, he thought; who ever got emotional over Welfare Island?

But the islands, the two he visited, let him down. Freeman walked off the vaporetto at Isola Bella amid a crowd of late-season tourists in all languages, especially German, who were at once beset by many vendors of cheap trinkets. And he discovered there were guided tours only – strictly no unsupervised wandering – the pink palazzo full of old junk, surrounded by artificial formal gardens, including grottoes made of seashells, the stone statuary a tasteless laugh. And although Isola dei Pescatori had some honest atmosphere, old houses hugging crooked streets, thick nets drying in piles near fishermen's dories drawn up among trees; again there were tourists snapping all in pictures, and the whole town catering to them. Everybody had something to sell you could buy better in Macy's basement. Freeman returned to his pensione, disappointed. The islands, beautiful from afar, up close were so much stage scenery. He complained thus to the padrona and she urged him to visit Isola del Dongo. 'More natural,' she persuaded him. 'You never saw such unusual gardens. And the palazzo is historical, full of the tombs of famous men of the region, including a cardinal who became a saint. Napoleon, the emperor, slept there. The French have always loved this island. Their writers have wept at its beauty.'

However, Freeman showed little interest. 'Gardens I've seen in my time.' So when restive, he wandered in the back streets of Stresa, watching the men playing at boccia, avoiding the laden store windows. Drifting by devious routes back to the lake, he sat at a bench in the small park, watching the lingering sunset over the dark mountains and thinking of a life of adventure. He watched alone, talked now and then to stray Italians – almost everybody spoke a good broken English – and lived too much on himself. On weekends, there was, however, a buzz of merriment in the streets. Excursionists from around Milan arrived in busloads. All day they hurried to their picnics; at night one of them pulled an accordion out of the bus and played sad Venetian or happy Neapolitan songs. Then the young Italians and their girls got up and danced in tight embrace in the public square; but not Freeman.

One evening at sunset, the calm waters so marvellously painted they drew him from inactivity, he hired a rowboat, and for want of any place more exciting to go, rowed towards the Isola del Dongo. He had no intention other than reaching it, then turning back, a round trip completed. Two-thirds of the way there, he began to row with growing uneasiness which soon became dread, because a stiff breeze had risen, driving the sucking waves against the side of the boat. It was a warm wind, but a wind was a wind and the water was wet. Freeman didn't row well – had learned late in his twenties, despite the nearness of Central Park – and he swam poorly, always swallowing water, never enough breath to get anywhere; clearly a landlubber from the word go. He strongly considered returning to Stresa – it was at least a half mile to the island, then a mile and a half in return – but chided himself for his timidity. He had, after all, hired the boat for an hour; so he kept rowing though he feared the risk. However, the waves were not too bad and he had discovered the trick of letting them hit the prow head-on. Although he handled his oars awkwardly, Freeman, to his surprise, made good time. The wind now helped rather than hindered; and daylight – reassuring – still lingered in the sky among streaks of red.

At last Freeman neared the island. Like Isola Bella, it rose in terraces through hedged gardens crowded with statuary, to a palazzo on top. But the padrona had told the truth – this island looked more interesting than the others, the vegetation lush, wilder, exotic birds flying around. By now the place was bathed in mist, and despite the thickening dark, Freeman recaptured the sense of awe and beauty he had felt upon first beholding the islands. At the same time he recalled a sad memory of unlived life, his own, of all that had slipped through his fingers. Amidst these thoughts he was startled by a movement in the garden by the water's edge. It had momentarily seemed as though a statue had come to life, but Freeman quickly realized a woman was standing this side of a low marble wall, watching the water. He could not, of course, make out her face, though he sensed she was young; only the skirt of her white dress moved in the breeze. He imagined someone waiting for her lover, and was tempted to speak to her, but then the wind blew up strongly and the waves rocked his rowboat. Freeman hastily turned the boat with one oar, and pulling hard, took off. The wind drenched him with spray, the rowboat bobbed among nasty waves, the going grew frighteningly rough. He had visions of drowning, the rowboat swamped, poor Freeman slowly sinking to the bottom, striving fruitlessly to reach the top. But as he rowed, his heart like a metal disc in his mouth, and still rowed on, gradually he overcame his fears; also the waves and wind. Although the lake was by now black, though the sky still dimly reflected white, turning from time to time to peer ahead, he guided himself by the flickering lights of the Stresa shore. It rained hard as he landed, but Freeman, as he beached the boat, considered his adventure an accomplishment and ate a hearty supper at an expensive restaurant.

The curtains billowing in his sunny room the next morning awoke him. Freeman rose, shaved, bathed, and after breakfast got a haircut. Wearing his bathing trunks under slacks, he sneaked on to the Hotel Excelsior beach for a dip, short but refreshing. In the early afternoon he read his Italian lesson on the balcony, then snatched a snooze. At four-thirty – he felt he really hadn't made up his mind until then – Freeman boarded the vaporetto making its hourly tour of the islands. After touching at Isola Madre, the boat headed for the Isola del Dongo. As they were approaching the island, coming from the direction opposite that which Freeman had taken last night, he observed a lanky boy in bathing trunks sunning himself on a raft in the lake – nobody he recognized. When the vaporetto landed at the dock on the southern side of the island, to Freeman's surprise and deep regret, the area was crowded with the usual stalls piled high with tourist gewgaws. And though he had hoped otherwise, inspection of the island was strictly in the guide's footsteps, and *vietato* trying to go anywhere alone. You paid a hundred lire for a ticket, then trailed behind this unshaven sad-looking clown, who stabbed a jaunty cane at the sky as he announced in three languages to the tourists who followed him : 'Please not stray nor wander. The family del Dongo, one of the most illustrious of Italy, so requests. Only thus ees eet able to remain open thees magnificent 'eestorical palatz and supreme jardens for the inspection by the members of all nations.'

They tailed the guide at a fast clip through the palace, through long halls hung with tapestries and elaborate mirrors, enormous rooms filled with antique furniture, old books, paintings, statuary – a lot of it in better taste than the stuff he had seen on the other island; and he visited where Napoleon had slept – a bed. Yet Freeman secretly touched the counterpane, though not quickly enough to escape the all-seeing eye of the Italian guide, who wrathfully raised his cane to the

level of Freeman's heart and explosively shouted, 'Basta !' This
embarrassed Freeman and two British ladies carrying parasols.
He felt bad until the group – about twenty – were led into
the garden. Gazing from here, the highest point of the island,
at the panorama of the golden-blue lake, Freeman gasped.
And the luxuriant vegetation of the island was daring, volup-
tuous. They went among orange and lemon trees (he had
never known that lemon was a perfume), magnolia, oleander
– the guide called out the names. Everywhere were flowers in
great profusion, huge camellias, rhododendron, jasmine, roses
in innumerable colours and varieties, all bathed in intoxicat-
ing floral fragrance. Freeman's head swam; he felt dizzy,
slightly off his rocker at this extraordinary assailment of his
senses. At the same time, though it was an 'underground'
reaction, he experienced a painful, contracting remembrance –
more like a warning – of personal poverty. This he had difficulty accounting for, because he usually held a decent opinion
of himself. When the comical guide bounced forward, with
his cane indicating cedars, eucalyptus, camphor and pepper
trees, the former floorwalker, overcome by all he was for the
first time seeing, at the same moment choked by almost breathless excitement, fell behind the group of tourists, and pretended to inspect the berries of a pepper tree. As the guide
hurried forward, Freeman, although not positive he had
planned it so, ducked behind the pepper tree, ran along a path
beside a tall laurel shrub and down two flights of stairs; he
hopped over a marble wall and went hastily through a small
wood, expectant, seeking, he thought only God knew what.

He figured he was headed in the direction of the garden by
the water where he had seen the girl in the white dress last
night, but after several minutes of involved wandering, Freeman came upon a little beach, a pebbly strand, leading down
stone steps into the lake. About a hundred feet away a raft
was anchored, nobody on it. Exhausted by the excitement, a
little moody, Freeman sat down under a tree, to rest. When he
glanced up, a girl in a white bathing suit was coming up the
steps out of the water. Freeman stared as she sloshed up the

shore, her wet skin glistening in bright sunlight. She had seen
him and quickly bent for a towel she had left on a blanket,
draped it over her shoulders and modestly held the ends together over her high-arched breast. Her wet black hair fell
upon her shoulders. She stared at Freeman. He rose, forming
words of apology in his mind. A haze that had been before his
eyes, evaporated. Freeman grew pale and the girl blushed.

Freeman was, of course, a New York City boy from away
back. As the girl stood there unselfconsciously regarding him
– it could not have been longer than thirty seconds – he was
aware of his background and certain other disadvantages; but
he also knew he wasn't a bad-looking guy, even, it could be
said, quite on the handsome side. Though a pinprick bald
at the back of his noggin – not more than a dime could
adequately cover – his head of hair was alive, expressive; Freeman's grey eyes were clear, unenvious, nose well-moulded, the
mouth generous. He had well-proportioned arms and legs and
his stomach lay respectfully flat. He was a bit short, but on
him, he knew, it barely showed. One of his former girl friends
had told him she sometimes thought of him as tall. This
counterbalanced the occasions when he had thought of himself as short. Yet though he knew he made a good appearance,
Freeman feared this moment, partly because of all he hun-
gered for from life, and partly because of the uncountable
obstacles existing between strangers, may the word for ever
perish.

She, apparently, had no fear of their meeting; as a matter of
surprising fact, seemed to welcome it, immediately curious
about him. She had, of course, the advantage of position –
which included receiving, so to speak, the guest-intruder. And
she had grace to lean on; herself also favoured physically –
mama, what a queenly high-assed form – itself the cause of
grace. Her dark, sharp Italian face had that quality of beauty
which holds the mark of history, the beauty of people and
civilization. The large brown eyes, under straight slender
brows, were filled with sweet light; her lips were purely cut as
if from red flowers; her nose was perhaps the one touch of

imperfection that perfected the rest – a trifle long and thin.
Despite the effect, a little of sculpture, her ovoid face, taper-
ing to a small chin, was soft, suffused with the loveliness of
youth. She was about twenty-three or -four. And when Freeman had, to a small degree, calmed down, he discovered in her
eyes a hidden hunger, or memory thereof; perhaps it was
sadness; and he felt he was, for this reason, if not unknown
others, sincerely welcomed. Had he, Oh God, at last met his
fate?

'Si è perduto?' the girl asked, smiling, still tightly holding
her white towel. Freeman understood and answered in English. 'No, I came on my own. On purpose you might say.' He
had in mind to ask her if she remembered having seen him
before, namely in last night's rowboat, but didn't.

'Are you an American?' she inquired, her Italian accent
pleasantly touched with an English one.

'That's right.'

The girl studied him for a full minute, and then hesitantly
asked, 'Are you, perhaps, Jewish?'

Freeman suppressed a groan. Though secretly shocked by
the question, it was not, in a way, unexpected. Yet he did not
look Jewish, could pass as not – had. So without batting an
eyelash, he said, no, he wasn't. And a moment later added,
though he personally had nothing against them.

'It was just a thought. You Americans are so varied,' she
explained vaguely.

'I understand,' he said, 'but have no worry.' Lifting his
hat, he introduced himself: 'Henry R. Freeman, travelling
abroad.'

'My name,' she said, after an absent-minded pause, 'is
Isabella del Dongo.'

Safe on first, thought Freeman. 'I'm proud to know you.'
He bowed. She gave him her hand with a gentle smile. He was
about to surprise it with a kiss when the comical guide appeared at a wall a few terraces above. He gazed at them in
astonishment, then let out a yell and ran down the stairs,
waving his cane like a rapier.

'Transgressor,' he shouted at Freeman.

The girl said something to calm him, but the guide was too furious to listen. He grabbed Freeman's arm, yanking him towards the stairs. And though Freeman, in the interest of good manners, barely resisted, the guide whacked him across the seat of the pants; but the ex-floorwalker did not complain.

Though his departure from the island had been, to put it mildly, an embarrassment (the girl had vanished after her unsuccessful momentary intercession), Freeman dreamed of a triumphant return. The big thing so far was that she, a knockout, had taken to him; he had been favoured by her. Just why, he couldn't exactly tell, but he could tell yes, had seen in her eyes. Yet wondering if yes why yes – an old habit – Freeman, among other reasons he had already thought of, namely the thus and therefore of man-woman attraction – laid it to the fact that he was different, had dared. He had, specifically, dared to duck the guide and be waiting for her at the edge of the lake when she came out of it. And she was different too, (which of course quickened her response to him). Not only in her looks and background, but of course different as regards past. (He had been reading with fascination about the del Dongos in all the local guide books.) Her past he could see boiling in her all the way back to the knights of old, and then some; his own history was something else again, but men were malleable, and he wasn't afraid of attempting to create certain daring combinations: Isabella and Henry Freeman. Hoping to meet someone like her was his main reason for having come abroad. And he had also felt he would be appreciated more by a European woman; his personality, that is. Yet, since their lives were so different, Freeman had moments of grave doubt, wondered what trials he was in for if he went after her, as he had every intention of doing: with her unknown family – other things of that sort. And he was in afterthought worried because she had asked him if he was Jewish. Why had the question popped out of her pretty mouth before they had even met? He had never before been asked anything like this by a girl, under let's call it similar circumstances. Just when they were looking each other over. He was puzzled because he absolutely did not look Jewish. But then he figured her question might have been a 'test' of some kind, she making it a point, when a man attracted her, quickly to determine his 'eligibility'. Maybe she had once had some sort of unhappy experience with a Jew? Unlikely, but possible, they were now everywhere. Freeman finally explained it to himself as 'one of those things', perhaps a queer thought that had for no good reason impulsively entered her mind. And because it was queer, his answer, without elaboration, was sufficient. With ancient history why bother? All these things – the odds against him, whetted his adventurous appetite.

He was in the grip of an almost unbearable excitement and must see her again soon, often, become her friend – not more than a beginning but where begin? He considered calling her on the telephone, if there was one in a palazzo where Napoleon had slept. But if the maid or somebody answered the phone first, he would have a ridiculous time identifying himself so he settled for sending her a note. Freeman wrote a few lines on good stationery he had bought for the purpose, asking if he might have the pleasure of seeing her again under circumstances favourable to leisurely conversation. He suggested a carriage ride to one of the other lakes in the neighbourhood, and signed his name not Levin, of course, but Freeman. Later he told the padrona that anything addressed to that name was meant for him. She was always to refer to him as Mr Freeman. He gave no explanation, although the padrona raised interested brows; but after he had slipped her – for reasons of friendship – a thousand lire, her expression became serene. Having mailed the letter, he felt time descend on him like an intricate trap. How would he ever endure until she answered? That evening he impatiently hired a rowboat and headed for Isola del Dongo. The water was glassy smooth but when he arrived, the palazzo was dark, almost gloomy, not a single window lit; the whole island looked dead. He saw no one, though he imagined her presence. Freeman thought of tying up at a dock and searching around a bit, but it seemed like folly. Row-

ing back to Stresa, he was stopped by the lake patrol and com-
pelled to show his passport. An officer advised him not to row
on the lake after dark; he might have an accident. The next
morning, wearing sunglasses, a light straw, recently pur-
chased, and a seersucker suit, he boarded the vaporetto and
soon landed on the island of his dreams, together with the
usual group of tourists. But the fanatic guide at once spied
Freeman, and waving his cane like a schoolmaster's rod, called
on him to depart peacefully. Fearing a scene that the girl would
surely hear of, Freeman left at once, greatly annoyed. The
padrona, that night, in a confidential mood, warned him not
to have anything to do with anybody on the Isola del Dongo.
The family had a perfidious history and was known for its
deceit and trickery.

On Sunday, at the low point of depression after an afternoon nap, Freeman heard a knock on his door. A long-legged
boy in short pants and a torn shirt handed him an envelope,
the corner embossed with somebody's coat of arms. Breathlessly, Freeman tore it open and extracted a sheet of thin bluish
paper with a few lines of spidery writing on it : 'You may come
this afternoon at six. Ernesto will accompany you. I. del D.'
It was already after five. Freeman was overwhelmed, giddy
with pleasure

'Tu sei Ernesto?' he asked the boy.

The boy, perhaps eleven or twelve, who had been watching
Freeman with large curious eyes, shook his head. 'No, Signore.
Sono Giacobbe.'

'Dov'è Ernesto?'

The boy pointed vaguely at the window, which Freeman
took to mean that whoever he was was waiting at the lake
front.

Freeman changed in the bathroom, emerging in a jiffy with
his new straw hat on and the seersucker suit. 'Let's go.' He
ran down the stairs, the boy running after him.

At the dock, to Freeman's startled surprise, 'Ernesto'
turned out to be the temperamental guide with the pestif-
erous cane, probably a major domo in the palazzo, long with

the family. Now a guide in another context, he was obviously an unwilling one, to judge from his expression. Perhaps a few wise words had subdued him and though haughty still, he settled for a show of politeness. Freeman greeted him courteously. The guide sat not in the ritzy launch Freeman had expected to see, but at the stern of an oversize, weather-beaten rowboat, a cross between a fishing dory and small life-boat. Preceded by the boy, Freeman climbed in over the unoccupied part of the rear seat, then, as Giacobbe took his place at the oars, hesitantly sat down next to Ernesto. One of the boatmen on the shore gave them a shove off and the boy began to row. The big boat seemed hard to manoeuvre, but Giacobbe, working deftly with a pair of long, heavy oars, managed with ease. He rowed quickly from the shore and towards the island where Isabella was waiting.

Freeman, though heartened to be off, contented, loving the wide airy world, wasn't comfortable sitting so snug with Ernesto, who smelled freshly of garlic. The talkative guide was a silent traveller. A dead cheroot hung from the corner of his mouth, and from time to time he absently poked his cane in the slats at the bottom of the boat; if there was no leak, Freeman thought, he would create one. He seemed tired, as if he had been carousing all night and had found no time to rest. Once he removed his black felt hat to mop his head with a handkerchief, and Freeman realized he was bald and looked surprisingly old.

Though tempted to say something pleasant to the old man – no hard feelings on this marvellous journey, Freeman had no idea where to begin. What would he reply to a grunt? After a time of prolonged silence, now a bit on edge, Freeman remarked, 'Maybe I'd better row and give the boy a rest?'

'As you weesh.' Ernesto shrugged.

Freeman traded places with the boy, then wished he hadn't. The oars were impossibly heavy; he rowed badly, allowing the left oar to sink deeper into the water than the right, thus twisting the boat off course. It was like pulling a hearse, and as he awkwardly splashed the oars around, he was embarrassedly aware of the boy and Ernesto, alike in their dark eyes and greedy beaks, a pair of odd birds, openly staring at him. He wished them far far away from the beautiful island and in exasperation pulled harder. By dint of determined effort, though his palms were painfully blistered, he began to row rhythmically, and the boat went along more smoothly. Freeman gazed up in triumph but they were no longer watching him, the boy trailing a straw in the water, the guide staring dreamily into the distance.

After a while, as if having studied Freeman and decided, when all was said and done, that he wasn't exactly a villain, Ernesto spoke in a not unfriendly tone.

'Everybody says how reech ees America?' he remarked.

'Rich enough,' Freeman grunted.

'Also thees ees the same with you?' The guide spoke with a half-embarrassed smile around his drooping cheroot butt.

'I'm comfortable,' Freeman replied, and in honesty added, 'but I have to work for a living.'

'For the young people ees a nice life, no? I mean there ees always what to eat, and for the woman een the house many remarkable machines?'

'Many,' Freeman said. Nothing comes from nothing, he thought. He's been asked to ask questions. Freeman then gave the guide an earful on the American standard of living, and he meant living. This for whatever it was worth to such as the Italian aristocracy. He hoped for the best. You could never tell the needs and desires of others.

Ernesto, as if memorizing what he had just heard, watched Freeman row for a while.

'Are you in biziness?' he ultimately asked.

Freeman searched around and came up with, 'Sort of in public relations.'

Ernesto now threw away his butt. 'Excuse me that I ask. How much does one earn in thees biziness in America?'

Calculating quickly, Freeman replied, 'I personally average about a hundred dollars a week. That comes to about a quarter million lire every month.'

Ernesto repeated the sum, holding onto his hat in the breeze. The boy's eyes had widened. Freeman hid a satisfied smile.

'And your father?' Here the guide paused, searching Freeman's face.

'What about him?' asked Freeman, tensing.

'What ees hees trade?'

'Was. He's dead – insurance.'

Ernesto removed his respectful hat, letting the sunlight bathe his bald head. They said nothing more until they had reached the island, then Freeman, consolidating possible gain, asked him in a complimentary tone where he had learned his English.

'Everywhere,' Ernesto replied, with a weary smile, and, Freeman, alert for each shift in prevailing wind, felt that if he hadn't made a bosom friend, he had at least softened an enemy; and that, on home grounds, was going good.

They landed and watched the boy tie up the boat; Freeman asked Ernesto where the signorina was. The guide, now looking bored by it all, pointed his cane at the top terraces, a sweeping gesture that seemed to take in the whole upper half of the luscious island. Freeman hoped the man would not insist on accompanying him and interfering with his meeting with the girl; but when he looked down from looking up without sighting Isabella, both Ernesto and Giacobbe had made themselves scarce. Leave it to the Italians at this sort of thing, Freeman thought.

Warning himself to be careful, tactful, he went quickly up the stairs. At each terrace he glanced around, then ran up to the next, his hat already in his hand. He found her, after wandering through profusions of flowers, where he had guessed she would be, alone in the garden behind the palazzo. She was sitting on an old stone bench near a little marble fountain, whose jets from the mouths of mocking elves sparkled in mellow sunlight.

Beholding her, the lovely face, sharply incised, yet soft in its femininity, the dark eyes pensive, her hair loosely knotted at the nape of her graceful neck, Freeman ached to his oar-blistered fingers. She was wearing a linen blouse of some soft shade of red that fell gently upon her breasts, and a long, slender black skirt; her tanned legs were without stockings; and on her narrow feet she wore sandals. As Freeman approached her, walking slowly to keep from loping, she brushed back a strand of hair, a gesture so beautiful it saddened him, because it was gone in the doing; and though Freeman, on this miraculous Sunday evening was aware of his indefatigable reality, he could not help thinking as he dwelt upon her lost gesture, that she might be as elusive as it, as evanescent; and so might this island be, and so, despite all the days he had lived through, good, bad and boring, that too often sneaked into his thoughts – so, indeed, might he today, tomorrow. He went towards her with a deep sense of the transitoriness of things, but this feeling was overwhelmed by one of pure joy when she rose to give him her hand

'Welcome,' Isabella said, blushing; she seemed happy, yet, in her manner, a little agitated to see him – perhaps one and the same thing – and he wanted then and there to embrace her but could not work up the nerve. Although he felt in her presence a fulfilment, as if they had already confessed love for one another, at the same time Freeman sensed an uneasiness in her which made him think, though he fought the idea, that they were far away from love; or at least were approaching it through opaque mystery. But that's what happened, Freeman, who had often been in love, told himself. Until you were lovers you were strangers.

In conversation he was at first formal. 'I thank you for your kind note. I have been looking forward to seeing you.'

She turned towards the palazzo. 'My people are out. They have gone to a wedding on another island. May I show you something of the palace?'

He was at this news both pleased and disappointed. He did not at the moment feel like meeting her family. Yet if she had presented him, it would have been a good sign.

They walked for a while in the garden, then Isabella took

Freeman's hand and led him through a heavy door into the large rococo palazzo.

'What would you care to see?'

Though he had superficially been through two floors of the building, wanting to be led by her, this close to him, Freeman replied, 'Whatever you want me to.'

She took him first to the chamber where Napoleon had slept. 'It wasn't Napoleon himself, who slept here,' Isabella explained. 'He slept on Isola Bella. His brother Joseph may have been here, or perhaps Pauline, with one of her lovers. No one is sure.'

'Oh ho, a trick,' said Freeman.

'We often pretend,' she remarked. 'This is a poor country.'

They entered the main picture gallery. Isabella pointed out the Titians, Tintorettos, Bellinis, making Freeman breathless; then at the door of the room she turned with an embarrassed smile and said that most of the paintings in the gallery were copies.

'Copies?' Freeman was shocked.

'Yes, although there are some fair originals from the Lombard school.'

'All the Titians are copies?'

'All.'

This slightly depressed him. 'What about the statuary – also copies?'

'For the most part.'

His face fell.'

'Is something the matter?'

'Only that I couldn't tell the fake from the real.'

'Oh, but many of the copies are exceedingly beautiful,' Isabella said. 'It would take an expert to tell they weren't originals.'

'I guess I've got a lot to learn,' Freeman said.

At this she squeezed his hand and he felt better.

But the tapestries, she remarked as they traversed the long hall hung with them, which darkened as the sun set, were genuine and valuable. They meant little to Freeman: long floor-to-ceiling, bluish-green fabrics of woodland scenes: stags, unicorns and tigers disporting themselves, though in one picture, the tiger killed the unicorn. Isabella hurried past this and led Freeman into a room he had not been in before, hung with tapestries of sombre scenes from the *Inferno*. One before which they stopped, was of a writhing leper, spotted from head to foot with pustulating sores which he tore at with his nails but the itch went on forever.

'What did he do to deserve his fate?' Freeman inquired.

'He falsely said he could fly.'

'For that you go to hell?'

She did not reply. The hall had become gloomily dark, so they left.

From the garden close by the beach where the raft was anchored, they watched the water turn all colours. Isabella had little to say about herself – she seemed to be quite often pensive – and Freeman, concerned with the complexities of the future, though his heart contained multitudes, found himself comparatively silent. When the night was complete, as the moon was rising, Isabella said she would be gone for a moment, and stepped behind a shrub. When she came forth, Freeman had this utterly amazing vision of her, naked, but before he could even focus his eyes on her flowerlike behind, she was already in the water, swimming for the raft. After an anguished consideration of could he swim that far or would he drown, Freeman eager to see her from up close (she was sitting on the raft, showing her breasts to the moon) shed his clothes behind the shrub where her delicate things lay, and walked down the stone steps into the warm water. He swam awkwardly, hating the picture he must make in her eyes, Apollo Belvedere slightly maimed; and still suffered visions of drowning in twelve feet of water. Or suppose she had to jump in to rescue him? However, nothing risked, nothing gained, so he splashed on and made the raft with breath to spare, his worries always greater than their cause.

But when he had pulled himself up on the raft, to his dismay, Isabella was no longer there. He caught a glimpse of her on the shore, darting behind the shrub. Nursing gloomy thoughts, Freeman rested a while, then, when he had sneezed twice and presupposed a nasty cold, jumped into the water and splashed his way back to the island. Isabella, already clothed, was waiting with a towel. She threw it to Freeman as he came up the steps, and withdrew while he dried himself and dressed. When he came forth in his seersucker, he offered salami, prosciutto, cheese, bread, and red wine, from a large platter delivered from the kitchen. Freeman, for a while angered at the runaround on the raft, relaxed with the wine and feeling of freshness after a bath. The mosquitoes behaved long enough for him to say he loved her. Isabella kissed him tenderly, then Ernesto and Giacobbe appeared and rowed him back to Stresa.

Monday morning Freeman didn't know what to do with himself. He awoke with restless memories, enormously potent, many satisfying, some burdensome; they ate him, he ate them. He felt he should somehow have made every minute with her better, hadn't begun to say half of what he had wanted – the kind of man he was, what they could get out of life together. And he regretted that he hadn't gotten quickly to the raft, still excited by what might have happened if he had reached it before she had left. But a memory was only a memory – you could forget, not change it. On the other hand, he was pleased, surprised by what he had accomplished: the evening alone with her, the trusting intimate sight of her beautiful body, her kiss, the unspoken promise of love. His desire for her was so splendid it hurt. He wandered through the afternoon, dreaming of her, staring often at the glittering islands in the opaque lake. By nightfall he was exhausted and went to sleep oppressed by all he had lived through.

It was strange, he thought, as he lay in bed waiting to sleep, that of all his buzzing worries he was worried most about one. If Isabella loved him, as he now felt she did or would before very long; with the strength of this love they could conquer their problems as they arose. He anticipated a good handful, stirred up, in all probability, by her family; but life in the

U.S.A. was considered by many Italians, including aristocrats (else why had Ernesto been sent to sniff out conditions there?) a fine thing for their marriageable daughters. Given this additional advantage, things would somehow get worked out, especially if Isabella, an independent girl, gazed a little eagerly at the star-spangled shore. Her family would give before flight in her eyes. No, the worry that troubled him most was the lie he had told her, that he wasn't a Jew. He could, of course, confess, say she knew Levin, not Freeman, man of adventure, but that might ruin all, since it was quite clear she wanted nothing to do with a Jew, or why, at first sight, had she asked so searching a question? Or he might admit nothing and let her, more or less, find out after she had lived a while in the States and seen it was no crime to be Jewish; that a man's past was, it could safely be said, expendable. Yet this treatment, if the surprise was upsetting, might cause recriminations later on. Another solution might be one he had thought of often: to change his name (he had considered Le Vin but preferred Freeman) and forget he had ever been born Jewish.

There was no question of hurting family, or being embarrassed by them, he the only son of both parents dead. Cousins lived in Toledo, Ohio, where they would always live and never bother. And when he brought Isabella to America they could skip N.Y.C. and go to live in a place like San Francisco, where nobody knew him and nobody 'would know'. To arrange such details and prepare other minor changes was why he figured on a trip or two home before they were married; he was prepared for that. As for the wedding itself, since he would have to marry her here to get her out of Italy, it would probably have to be in a church, but he would go along with that to hasten things. It was done every day. Thus he decided, although it did not entirely satisfy him; not so much the denial of being Jewish – what had it brought him but headaches, inferiorities, unhappy memories? – as the lie to the beloved. At first sight love and a lie; it lay on his heart like a sore. Yet, if that was the way it had to be, it was the way.

He awoke the next morning, beset by a swarm of doubts concerning his plans and possibilities. When would he see Isabella again, let alone marry her? ('When?' he had whispered before getting into the boat, and she had vaguely promised, 'Soon.') Soon was brutally endless. The mail brought nothing and Freeman grew dismayed. Had he, he asked himself, been constructing a hopeless fantasy, wish seducing probability? Was he inventing a situation that didn't exist, namely, her feeling for him, the possibility of a future with her? He was desperately casting about for something to keep his mood from turning dark blue, when a knock sounded on his door. The padrona, he thought, because she often came up for one unimportant thing or another, but to his unspeakable joy it was Cupid in short pants – Giacobbe holding forth the familiar envelope. She would meet him, Isabella wrote, at two o'clock in the piazza where the electric tram took off for Mt Mottarone, from whose summit one saw the beautiful panorama of lakes and mountains in the region. Would he share this with her?

Although he had quashed the morning's anxiety, Freeman was there at one p.m., smoking impatiently. His sun rose as she appeared, but as she came towards him he noticed she was not quite looking at him (in the distance he could see Giacobbe rowing away) her face neutral, inexpressive. He was at first concerned, but she had, after all, written the letter to him, so he wondered what hot nails she had had to walk on to get off the island. He must sometime during the day drop the word 'elope' to see if she savoured it. But whatever was bothering her, Isabella immediately shook off. She smiled as she greeted him; he hoped for her lips but got instead her polite fingers. These he kissed in broad daylight (let the spies tell papa) and she shyly withdrew her hand. She was wearing – it surprised him, though he gave her credit for resisting foolish pressures – exactly the same blouse and skirt she had worn on Sunday. They boarded the tram with a dozen tourists and sat alone on the open seat in front; as a reward for managing this she permitted Freeman to hold her hand. He sighed. The tram, drawn by an old electric locomotive moved slowly through the town and more slowly up the slope of the mountain. They rode for close to two hours, watching the lake fall as the mountains rose. Isabella, apart from pointing to something now and then, was again silent, withdrawn, but Freeman, allowing her her own rate at flowering, for a moment without plans, was practically contented. A long vote for an endless journey; but the tram at last came to a stop and they walked through a field thick with wildflowers, up the slope to the summit of the mountain. Though the tourists followed in a crowd, the mountain top was broad and they stood near its edge, to all intents and purposes alone. Below them, on the green undulating plains of Piedmont and Lombardy, seven lakes were scattered, each a mirror reflecting whose fate? And high in the distance rose a ring of astonishing snow-clad Alps. Ah, he murmured, and fell silent.

'We say here,' Isabella said, ' "un pezzo di paradiso caduto dal cielo." '

'You can say it again.' Freeman was deeply moved by the sublimity of the distant Alps. She named the white peaks from Mt Rosa to the Jungfrau. Gazing at them, he felt he had grown a head taller and was inspired to accomplish a feat men would wonder at.

'Isabella –' Freeman turned to ask her to marry him; but she was standing apart from him, her face pale.

Pointing to the snowy mountains, her hand moving in a gentle arc, she asked, 'Don't those peaks – those seven – look like a Menorah?'

'Like a what?' Freeman politely inquired. He had a sudden frightening remembrance of her seeing him naked as he came out of the lake and felt constrained to tell her that circumcision was de rigueur in stateside hospitals; but he didn't dare. She may not have noticed.

'Like a seven-branched candelabrum holding white candles in the sky?' Isabella asked.

'Something like that.'

'Or do you see the Virgin's crown adorned with jewels?'

'Maybe the crown,' he faltered. 'It all depends how you look at it.'

They left the mountain and went down to the water. The tram ride was faster going down. At the lake front, as they were waiting for Giacobbe to come with the rowboat, Isabella, her eyes troubled, told Freeman she had a confession to make. He, still eager to propose, hoped she would finally say she loved him. Instead, she said, 'My name is not del Dongo. It is Isabella della Seta. The del Dongos have not been on the island in years. We are the caretakers of the palace, my father, brother and I. We are poor people.'

'Caretakers?' Freeman was astonished.

'Yes.'

'Ernesto is your father?' His voice rose.

She nodded.

'Was it his idea for you to say you were somebody else?'

'No, mine. He did what I asked him to. He has wanted me to go to America, but under the right circumstances.'

'So you had to pretend,' he said bitterly. He was more greatly disturbed than he could account for, as if he had been expecting just this to happen.

She blushed and turned away. 'I was not sure of the circumstances. I wanted you to stay until I knew you better.'

'Why didn't you say so?'

'Perhaps I wasn't serious in the beginning. I said what I thought you wanted to hear. At the same time I wished you to stay. I thought you would be clearer to me after a while.'

'Clearer how?'

'I don't really know.' Her eyes searched his, then she dropped her glance.

'I'm not hiding anything,' he said. He wanted to say more but warned himself not to.

'That's what I was afraid of.'

Giacobbe had come with the boat and steadied it for his sister. They were alike as the proverbial peas – two dark Italian faces, the Middle Ages looking out of their eyes. Isabella got into the boat and Giacobbe pushed off with one oar. She waved from afar.

Freeman went back to his pensione in a turmoil, hurt where it hurts – in his dreams, thinking he should have noticed before how worn her blouse and skirt were, should have seen more than he had. It was this that irked. He called himself a damn fool for making up fairy tales – Freeman in love with the Italian aristocracy. He thought of taking off for Venice or Florence, but his heart ached for love of her, and he could not forget that he had originally come in the simple hope of finding a girl worth marrying. If the desire had developed complications, the fault was mostly his own. After an hour in his room, burdened by an overpowering loneliness, Freeman felt he must have her. She mustn't get away from him. So what if the countess had become a caretaker? She was a natural-born queen, whether by del Dongo or any other name. So she had lied to him, but so had he to her; they were quits on that score and his conscience was calm. He felt things would be easier all around now that the air had been cleared.

Freeman ran down to the dock; the sun had set and the boatmen were home, swallowing spaghetti. He was considering untying one of the rowboats and paying tomorrow, when he caught sight of someone sitting on a bench – Ernesto, in his hot winter hat, smoking a cheroot. He was resting his wrists on the handle of his cane, his chin on them.

'You weesh a boat?' the guide asked in a not unkindly tone.

'With all my heart. Did Isabella send you?'

'No.'

He came because she was unhappy, Freeman guessed – maybe crying. There's a father for you, a real magician despite his appearance. He waves his stick and up pops Freeman for his little girl.

'Get een,' said Ernesto.

'I'll row,' said Freeman. He had almost added 'father', but had caught himself. As if guessing the jest, Ernesto smiled, a little sadly. But he sat at the stern of the boat, enjoying the ride.

In the middle of the lake, seeing the mountains surrounding it lit in the last glow of daylight, Freeman thought of the 'Menorah' in the Alps. Where had she got the word, he wondered, and decided anywhere, a book or picture. But wherever she had, he must settle this subject once and for all tonight.

When the boat touched the dock, the pale moon rose. Ernesto tied up, and handed Freeman a flashlight.

'Een the jarden,' he said tiredly, pointing with his cane.

'Don't wait up.' Freeman hastened to the garden at the lake's edge, where the roots of trees hung like hoary beards above the water; the flashlight didn't work, but the moon and his memory were enough. Isabella, God bless her, was standing at the low wall among the moonlit statuary : stags, tigers and unicorns, poets and painters, shepherds with pipes, and playful shepherdesses, gazing at the light shimmering on the water.

She was wearing white, the figure of a future bride; perhaps it was an altered wedding dress – he would not be surprised if a hand-me-down, the way they saved clothes in this poor country. He had pleasant thoughts of buying her some nifty outfits.

She was motionless, her back towards him – though he could picture her bosom breathing. When he said good evening, lifting his light straw, she turned to him with a sweet smile. He tenderly kissed her lips; this she let him do, softly returning the same.

'Good-bye,' Isabella whispered.

'To whom good-bye?' Freeman affectionately mocked. 'I have come to marry you.'

She gazed at him with eyes moistly bright, then came the soft, inevitable thunder : 'Are you a Jew?'

'Why should I lie?' he thought; she's mine for the asking. But then he trembled with the fear of at the last moment losing her, so Freeman answered, though his scalp prickled, 'How many no's make never? Why do you persist with such foolish questions?'

'Because I hoped you were.' Slowly she unbuttoned her

bodice, arousing Freeman, though he was thoroughly confused as to her intent. When she revealed her breasts – he
could have wept at their beauty (now recalling a former in-
vitation to gaze at them, but he had arrived too late on the
raft) – to his horror he discerned tattooed on the soft and
tender flesh a bluish line of distorted numbers.

'Buchenwald,' Isabella said, 'when I was a little girl. The
Fascists sent us there. The Nazis did it.'

Freeman groaned, incensed at the cruelty, stunned by the
desecration.

'I can't marry you. We are Jews. My past is meaningful to
me. I treasure what I suffered for.'

'Jews,' he muttered, '– you? Oh, God, why did you keep
this from me, too?'

'I did not wish to tell you something you would not welcome. I thought at one time it was possible you were – I hoped
but was wrong.'

'Isabella –' he cried brokenly. 'Listen, I – I am –'

He groped for her breasts, to clutch, kiss or suckle them;
but she had stepped among the statues, and when he vainly
sought her in the veiled mist that had risen from the lake, still
calling her name, Freeman embraced only moonlit stone.

A Summer's Reading

George Stoyonovich was a neighbourhood boy who had quit high school on an impulse when he was sixteen, run out of patience, and though he was ashamed every time he went looking for a job, when people asked him if he had finished and he had to say no, he never went back to school. This summer was a hard time for jobs and he had none. Having so much time on his hands, George thought of going to summer school, but the kids in his classes would be too young. He also considered registering in a night high school, only he didn't like the idea of the teachers always telling him what to do. He felt they had not respected him. The result was he stayed off the streets and in his room most of the day. He was close to twenty and had needs with the neighbourhood girls, but no money to spend, and he couldn't get more than an occasional few cents because his father was poor, and his sister Sophie, who resembled George, a tall bony girl of twenty-three, earned very little and what she had she kept for herself. Their mother was dead, and Sophie had to take care of the house.

Very early in the morning George's father got up to go to work in a fish market. Sophie left at about eight for her long ride in the subway to a cafeteria in the Bronx. George had his coffee by himself, then hung around in the house. When the house, a five-room railroad flat above a butcher store, got on his nerves he cleaned it up – mopped the floors with a wet mop and put things away. But most of the time he sat in his room. In the afternoons he listened to the ball game. Otherwise he had a couple of old copies of the *World Almanac* he had bought long ago, and he liked to read in them and also the magazines and newspapers that Sophie brought home, that had been left on the tables in the cafeteria. They were mostly picture magazines about movie stars and sports figures, also usually the *News* and *Mirror*. Sophie herself read whatever fell into her hands, although she sometimes read good books.

She once asked George what he did in his room all day and he said he read a lot too.

'Of what besides what I bring home? Do you ever read any worthwhile books?'

'Some,' George answered, although he really didn't. He had tried to read a book or two that Sophie had in the house but found he was in no mood for them. Lately he couldn't stand made-up stories, they got on his nerves. He wished he had some hobby to work at – as a kid he was good in carpentry, but where could he work at it? Sometimes during the day he went for walks, but mostly he did his walking after the hot sun had gone down and it was cooler in the streets.

In the evening after supper George left the house and wandered in the neighbourhood. During the sultry days some of the storekeepers and their wives sat in chairs on the thick, broken sidewalks in front of their shops, fanning themselves, and George walked past them and the guys hanging out on the candy store corner. A couple of them he had known his whole life, but nobody recognized each other. He had no place special to go, but generally, saving it till the last, he left the neighbourhood and walked for blocks till he came to a darkly lit little park with benches and trees and an iron railing, giving it a feeling of privacy. He sat on a bench here, watching the leafy trees and the flowers blooming on the inside of the railing, thinking of a better life for himself. He thought of the jobs he had had since he had quit school – delivery boy, stock clerk, runner, lately working in a factory – and he was dissatisfied with all of them. He felt he would some day like to have a job and live in a private house with a porch, on a street with trees. He wanted to have some dough in his pocket to buy things with, and a girl to go with, so as not to be lonely, especially on Saturday nights. He wanted people to like and respect him. He thought about these things often but mostly when he was alone at night. Around midnight he got up and drifted back to his hot and stony neighbourhood.

One time while on his walk George met Mr Cattanzara coming home very late from work. He wondered if he was drunk but then could tell he wasn't. Mr Cattanzara, a stocky, bald-headed man who worked in a change booth on an IRT station, lived on the next block after George's, above a shoe repair store. Nights, during the hot weather, he sat on his stoop in an undershirt, reading the *New York Times* in the light of the shoemaker's window. He read it from the first page to the last, then went up to sleep. And all the time he was reading the paper, his wife, a fat woman with a white face, leaned out of the window, gazing into the street, her thick white arms folded under her loose breast, on the window ledge.

Once in a while Mr Cattanzara came home drunk, but it was a quiet drunk. He never made any trouble, only walked stiffly up the street and slowly climbed the stairs into the hall. Though drunk, he looked the same as always, except for his tight walk, the quietness, and that his eyes were wet. George liked Mr Cattanzara because he remembered him giving him nickels to buy lemon ice with when he was a squirt. Mr Cattanzara was a different type than those in the neighbourhood. He asked different questions than the others when he met you, and he seemed to know what went on in all the newspapers. He read them, as his fat sick wife watched from the window.

'What are you doing with yourself this summer, George?' Mr Cattanzara asked. 'I see you walkin' around at nights.'

George felt embarrassed. 'I like to walk.'

'What are you doin' in the day now?'

'Nothing much just right now. I'm waiting for a job.' Since it shamed him to admit he wasn't working, George said, 'I'm staying home – but I'm reading a lot to pick up my education.'

Mr Cattanzara looked interested. He mopped his hot face with a red handkerchief.

'What are you readin'?'

George hesitated, then said, 'I got a list of books in the library once, and now I'm gonna read them this summer.' He felt strange and a little unhappy saying this, but he wanted Mr Cattanzara to respect him.

'How many books are there on it?'

'I never counted them. Maybe around a hundred.'

Mr Cattanzara whistled through his teeth.

'I figure if I did that,' George went on earnestly, 'it would help me in my education. I don't mean the kind they give you in high school. I want to know different things than they learn there, if you know what I mean.'

The change maker nodded. 'Still and all, one hundred books is a pretty big load for one summer.'

'It might take longer.'

'After you're finished with some, maybe you and I can shoot the breeze about them?' said Mr Cattanzara.

'When I'm finished,' George answered.

Mr Cattanzara went home and George continued on his walk. After that, though he had the urge to, George did nothing different from usual. He still took his walks at night, ending up in the little park. But one evening the shoemaker on the next block stopped George to say he was a good boy, and George figured that Mr Cattanzara had told him all about the books he was reading. From the shoemaker it must have gone down the street, because George saw a couple of people smiling kindly at him, though nobody spoke to him personally. He felt a little better around the neighbourhood and liked it more, though not so much he would want to live in it for ever. He had never exactly disliked the people in it, yet he had never liked them very much either. It was the fault of the neighbourhood. To his surprise, George found out that his father and Sophie knew about his reading too. His father was too shy to say anything about it – he was never much of a talker in his whole life – but Sophie was softer to George, and she showed him in other ways she was proud of him.

As the summer went on George felt in a good mood about

things. He cleaned the house every day, as a favour to Sophie, and he enjoyed the ball games more. Sophie gave him a buck a week allowance, and though it still wasn't enough and he had to use it carefully, it was a helluva lot better than just having two bits now and then. What he bought with the money – cigarettes mostly, an occasional beer or movie ticket – he got a big kick out of. Life wasn't so bad if you knew how to appreciate it. Occasionally he bought a paperback book from the news-stand, but he never got around to reading it, though he was glad to have a couple of books in his room. But he read thoroughly Sophie's magazines and newspapers. And at night was the most enjoyable time, because when he passed the storekeepers sitting outside their stores, he could tell they regarded him highly. He walked erect, and though he did not say much to them, or they to him, he could feel approval on all sides. A couple of nights he felt so good that he skipped the park at the end of the evening. He just wandered in the neighbourhood, where people had known him from the time he was a kid playing punchball whenever there was a game of it going; he wandered there, then came home and got undressed for bed, feeling fine.

For a few weeks he had talked only once with Mr Cattanzara, and though the change maker had said nothing more about the books, asked no questions, his silence made George a little uneasy. For a while George didn't pass in front of Mr Cattanzara's house any more, until one night, forgetting himself, he approached it from a different direction than he usually did when he did. It was already past midnight. The street, except for one or two people, was deserted, and George was surprised when he saw Mr Cattanzara still reading his newspaper by the light of the street lamp overhead. His impulse was to stop at the stoop and talk to him. He wasn't sure what he wanted to say, though he felt the words would come when he began to talk; but the more he thought about it, the more the idea scared him, and he decided he'd better not. He even considered beating it home by another street, but he was too near Mr Cattanzara, and the change maker might see him as he ran, and get annoyed. So George unobtrusively crossed the street, trying to make it seem as if he had to look in a store window on the other side, which he did, and then went on, uncomfortable at what he was doing. He feared Mr Cattanzara would glance up from his paper and call him a dirty rat for walking on the other side of the street, but all he did was sit there, sweating through his undershirt, his bald head shining in the dim light as he read his *Times*, and upstairs his fat wife leaned out of the window, seeming to read the paper along with him. George thought she would spy him and yell out to Mr Cattanzara, but she never moved her eyes off her husband.

George made up his mind to stay away from the change maker until he had got some of his softback books read, but when he started them and saw they were mostly story books, he lost his interest and didn't bother to finish them. He lost his interest in reading other things too. Sophie's magazines and newspapers went unread. She saw them piling up on a chair in his room and asked why he was no longer looking at them, and George told her it was because of all the other reading he had to do. Sophie said she had guessed that was it. So for most of the day, George had the radio on, turning to music when he was sick of the human voice. He kept the house fairly neat, and Sophie said nothing on the days when he neglected it. She was still kind and gave him his extra buck, though things weren't so good for him as they had been before.

But they were good enough, considering. Also his night walks invariably picked him up, no matter how bad the day was. Then one night George saw Mr Cattanzara coming down the street towards him. George was about to turn and run but he recognized from Mr Cattanzara's walk that he was drunk, and if so, probably he would not even bother to notice him. So George kept on walking straight ahead until he came abreast of Mr Cattanzara and though he felt wound up enough to pop into the sky, he was not surprised when Mr Cattanzara passed him without a word, walking slowly, his face and body stiff. George drew a breath in relief at his narrow escape, when he heard his name called, and there stood Mr Cattanzara at his elbow, smelling like the inside of a beer barrel. His eyes were sad as he gazed at George, and George felt so intensely uncomfortable he was tempted to shove the drunk aside and continue on his walk.

But he couldn't act that way to him, and, besides, Mr Cattanzara took a nickel out of his pants pocket and handed it to him.

'Go buy yourself a lemon ice, Georgie.'

'It's not that time any more, Mr Cattanzara,' George said, 'I am a big guy now.'

'No, you ain't,' said Mr Cattanzara, to which George made no reply he could think of.

'How are all your books comin' along now?' Mr Cattanzara asked. Though he tried to stand steady, he swayed a little.

'Fine, I guess,' said George, feeling the red crawling up his face.

'You ain't sure?' The change maker smiled slyly, a way George had never seen him smile.

'Sure I'm sure. They're fine.'

Though his head swayed in little arcs, Mr Cattanzara's eyes were steady. He had small blue eyes which could hurt if you looked at them too long.

'George,' he said, 'name me one book on that list that you read this summer, and I will drink to your health.'

'I don't want anybody drinking to me.'

'Name me one so I can ask you a question on it. Who can tell, if it's a good book maybe I might wanna read it myself.'

George knew he looked passable on the outside, but inside he was crumbling apart.

Unable to reply, he shut his eyes, but when – years later – he opened them, he saw that Mr Cattanzara had, out of pity, gone away, but in his ears he still heard the words he had said when he left: 'George, don't do what I did.'

The next night he was afraid to leave his room, and though Sophie argued with him he wouldn't open the door.

'What are you doing in there?' she asked.

'Nothing.'

'Are you reading?'

'No.'

She was silent a minute, then asked, 'Where do you keep the books you read? I never see any in your room outside of a few cheap trashy ones.'

He wouldn't tell her.

'In that case you're not worth a buck of my hard-earned money. Why should I break my back for you? Go on out, you bum, and get a job.'

He stayed in his room for almost a week, except to sneak into the kitchen when nobody was home. Sophie railed at him, then begged him to come out, and his old father wept, but George wouldn't budge, though the weather was terrible and his small room stifling. He found it very hard to breathe, each breath was like drawing a flame into his lungs.

One night, unable to stand the heat any more, he burst into the street at one a.m., a shadow of himself. He hoped to sneak to the park without being seen, but there were people all over the block, wilted and listless, waiting for a breeze. George lowered his eyes and walked, in disgrace, away from them, but before long he discovered they were still friendly to him. He figured Mr Cattanzara hadn't told on him. Maybe when he woke up out of his drunk the next morning, he had forgotten all about meeting George. George felt his confidence slowly come back to him.

That same night a man on a street corner asked him if it was true that he had finished reading so many books, and George admitted he had. The man said it was a wonderful thing for a boy his age to read so much.

'Yeah,' George said, but he felt relieved. He hoped nobody would mention the books any more, and when, after a couple of days, he accidentally met Mr Cattanzara again, *he* didn't, though George had the idea he was the one who had started the rumour that he had finished all the books.

One evening in the fall, George ran out of his house to the library, where he hadn't been in years. There were books all over the place, wherever he looked, and though he was struggling to control an inward trembling, he easily counted off a hundred, then sat down at a table to read.

The Bill

Though the street was somewhere near a river, it was land-locked and narrow, a crooked row of aged brick tenement buildings. A child throwing a ball straight up saw a bit of pale sky. On the corner, opposite the blackened tenement where Willy Schlegel worked as janitor, stood another like it except that this included the only store on the street – going down five stone steps into the basement, a small, dark deli-catessen owned by Mr and Mrs F. Panessa, really a hole in the wall.

They had just bought it with the last of their money, Mrs Panessa told the janitor's wife, so as not to have to depend on either of their daughters, both of whom, Mrs Schlegel under-stood, were married to selfish men who had badly affected their characters. To be completely independent of them, Panessa, a retired factory worker, withdrew his three thousands of sav-ings and bought this little delicatessen store. When Mrs Schlegel, looking around – though she knew the delicatessen quite well for the many years she and Willy had been janitors across the way – when she asked, 'Why did you buy this one?' Mrs Panessa cheerfully replied because it was a small place and they would not have to overwork; Panessa was sixty-three. They were not here to coin money but to support themselves without working too hard. After talking it over many nights and days, they had decided that the store would at least give them a living. She gazed into Etta Schlegel's gaunt eyes and Etta said she hoped so.

She told Willy about the new people across the street who had bought out the Jew, and said to buy there if there were a chance; she meant by that they would continue to shop at the self-service, but when there was some odd or end to pick up, or something they had forgotten to buy, they could go to Panessa's. Willy did as he was told. He was tall and broad-backed, with a heavy face seamed dark from the coal and ashes he shovelled around all winter, and his hair often looked grey from the dust the wind whirled up at him out of the ash cans when he was lining them up for the sanitation truck. Al-ways in overalls – he complained he never stopped working – he would drift across the street and down the steps when something was needed, and lighting his pipe, would stand around talking to Mrs Panessa as her husband, a small bent man with a fitful smile, stood behind the counter waiting for the janitor after a long interval of talk to ask, upon reflection, for a dime's worth of this or that, the whole business never amounting to more than half a dollar. Then one day Willy got to talking about how the tenants goaded him all the time and what the cruel and stingy landlord could think up for him to do in that smelly five-floor dungeon. He was absorbed by what he was saying and before he knew it had run up a three-dol-lar order, though all he had on him was fifty cents. Willy looked like a dog that had just had a licking, but Mr Panessa, after clearing his throat, chirped up it didn't matter, he could pay the rest whenever he wanted. He said that everything was run on credit, business and everything else, because after all what was credit but the fact that people were human beings, and if you were really a human being you gave credit to some-body else and he gave credit to you. That surprised Willy be-cause he had never heard a storekeeper say it before. After a couple of days he paid the two fifty, but when Panessa said he could trust whenever he felt like it, Willy sucked a flame into his pipe, then began to order all sorts of things.

When he brought home two large bagfuls of stuff, Etta shouted he must be crazy. Willy answered he had charged everything and paid no cash.

'But we have to pay sometime, don't we?' Etta shouted. 'And we have to pay higher prices than in the self-service.'

She said then what she always said, 'We're poor people, Willy. We can't afford too much.'

Though Willy saw the justice of her remarks, despite her scolding he still went across the street and trusted. Once he had a crumpled ten-dollar bill in his pants pocket and the amount came to less than four, but he didn't offer to pay, and let Panessa write it in the book. Etta knew he had the money so she screamed when he admitted he had bought on credit.

'Why are you doing it for? Why don't you pay if you have the money?'

He didn't answer but after a time he said there were other things he had to buy once in a while. He went into the furnace room and came out with a wrapped package which he opened, and it contained a beaded black dress.

Etta cried over the dress and said she would never wear it because the only time he ever brought her anything was when he had done something wrong. Thereafter she let him do all the grocery shopping and she did not speak when he bought on trust.

Willy continued to buy at Panessa's. It seemed they were always waiting for him to come in. They lived in three tiny rooms on the floor above the store, and when Mrs Panessa saw him out of her window, she ran down to the store. Willy came up from his basement, crossed the street and went down the steps into the delicatessen, looming large as he opened the door. Every time he bought, it was never less than two dollars' worth and sometimes it would go as high as five. Mrs Panessa would pack everything into a deep double bag, after Panessa had called off each item and written the price with a smeary black pencil into his looseleaf notebook. Whenever Willy walked in, Panessa would open the book, wet his finger tip and flip through a number of blank pages till he found Willy's account in the centre of the book. After the order was packed and tied up, Panessa added the amount, touching each figure with his pencil, hissing to himself as he added, and Mrs Panessa's bird eyes would follow the figuring until Panessa wrote down a sum, and the new total sum (after Panessa had glanced up at Willy and saw that Willy was looking) was twice underscored and then Panessa shut the book. Willy, with his loose unlit pipe in his mouth, did not move until the book was put away under the counter; then he roused himself and embracing the bundle – with which they offered to help him across the street though he always refused – plunged out of the store.

One day when the sum total came to eighty-three dollars and some cents, Panessa, lifting his head and smiling, asked Willy when he could pay something on account. The very next day Willy stopped buying at Panessa's and after that Etta, with her cord market bag, began to shop again at the self-service, and neither of them went across the street for as much as a pound of prunes or box of salt they had meant to buy but had forgotten.

Etta, when she returned from shopping at the self-service, scraped the wall on her side of the street to get as far away as possible from Panessa's.

Later she asked Willy if he had paid them anything.

He said no.

'When will you?'

He said he didn't know.

A month went by, then Etta met Mrs Panessa around the corner, and though Mrs Panessa, looking unhappy, said nothing about the bill, Etta came home and reminded Willy.

'Leave me alone,' he said, 'I got enough trouble of my own.'

'What kind of trouble have you got, Willy?'

'The goddam tenants and the goddam landlord,' he shouted and slammed the door.

When he returned he said, 'What have I got that I can pay? Ain't I been a poor man every day of my life?'

She was sitting at the table and lowered her arms and put her head down on them and wept.

'With what?' he shouted, his face lit up dark and webbed. 'With the meat off my bones?

'With the ashes in my eyes. With the piss I mop up on the floors. With the cold in my lungs when I sleep.'

He felt for Panessa and his wife a grating hatred and vowed never to pay because he hated them so much, especially the humpback behind the counter. If he ever smiled at him again with those goddam eyes he would lift him off the floor and crack his bent bones.

That night he went out and got drunk and lay till morning in the gutter. When he returned, with filthy clothes and bloodied eyes, Etta held up to him the picture of their four-year-old son who had died from diphtheria, and Willy weeping splashy tears, swore he would never touch another drop.

Each morning he went out to line up the ash cans, he never looked the full way across the street.

'Give credit,' he mimicked, 'give credit.'

Hard times set in. The landlord ordered cut down on heat, cut down on hot water. He cut down on Willy's expense money and wages. The tenants were angered. All day they pestered Willy like clusters of flies and he told them what the landlord had ordered. Then they cursed Willy and Willy cursed them. They telephoned the Board of Health but when the inspectors arrived they said the temperature was within the legal minimum though the house was draughty. However the tenants still complained they were cold and goaded Willy about it all day but he said he was cold too. He said he was freezing but no one believed him.

One day he looked up from lining up four ash cans for the truck to remove and saw Mr and Mrs Panessa staring at him from the store. They were staring up through the glass front door and when he looked at them at first his eyes blurred and they appeared to be two scrawny, loose-feathered birds.

He went down the block to get a wrench from another janitor, and when he got back they then reminded him of two skinny leafless bushes sprouting up through the wooden floor. He could see through the bushes to the empty shelves.

In the spring, when the grass shoots were sticking up from

the cracks in the sidewalk, he told Etta, 'I'm only waiting till I can pay it all.'

'How, Willy?'

'We can save up.'

'How?'

'How much do we save a month?'

'Nothing.'

'How much have you got hid away?'

'Nothing any more.'

'I'll pay them bit by bit. I will, by Jesus.'

The trouble was there was no place they could get the money. Sometimes when he was trying to think of the different ways there were to get money his thoughts ran ahead and he saw what it would be like when he paid. He would wrap up the wad of bills with a thick rubber band and then go up the stairs and cross the street and go down the five steps into the store. He would say to Panessa, 'Here it is, little old man, and I bet you didn't think I would do it, and I don't suppose nobody else did and sometimes me myself, but here it is in bucks all held together by a fat rubber band.' After hefting the wad a little, he placed it, like making a move on a checkerboard, squarely in the centre of the counter, and the diminutive man and his wife both unpeeled it, squeaking and squealing over each blackened buck, and marvelling that so many ones had been tied together into such a small pack.

Such was the dream Willy dreamed but he could never make it come true.

He worked hard to. He got up early and scrubbed the stairs from cellar to roof with soap and a hard brush then went over that with a wet mop. He cleaned the woodwork too and oiled the bannister till it shone the whole zigzag way down and rubbed the mailboxes in the vestibule with metal polish and a soft rag until you could see your face in them. He saw his own heavy face with a surprising yellow moustache he had recently grown and the tan felt cap he wore that a tenant had left behind in a closetful of junk when he had moved. Etta helped him and they cleaned the whole cellar and the dark courtyard under the crisscrossed clotheslines, and they were quick to respond to any kind of request, even from tenants they didn't like, for sink or toilet repairs. Both worked themselves to exhaustion every day, but as they knew from the beginning, no extra money came in.

One morning when Willy was shining up the mailboxes, he found in his own a letter for him. Removing his cap, he opened the envelope and held the paper to the light as he read the trembling writing. It was from Mrs Panessa, who wrote her husband was sick across the street, and she had no money in the house so could he pay her just ten dollars and the rest could wait for later.

He tore the letter into bits and hid all day in the cellar. That night, Etta, who had been searching for him in the streets, found him behind the furnace amid the pipes, and she asked him what he was doing there.

He explained about the letter.

'Hiding won't do you any good at all,' she said hopelessly.

'What should I do then?'

'Go to sleep, I guess.'

He went to sleep but the next morning burst out of his covers, pulled on his overalls and ran out of the house with an overcoat flung over his shoulders. Around the corner he found a pawnshop, where he got ten dollars for the coat and was gleeful.

But when he ran back, there was a hearse or something across the street, and two men in black were carrying this small and narrow pine box out of the house.

'Who's dead, a child?' he asked one of the tenants.

'No, a man named Mr Panessa.'

Willy couldn't speak. His throat had turned to bone.

After the pine box was squeezed through the vestibule doors, Mrs Panessa, grieved all over, tottered out alone. Willy turned his head away although he thought she wouldn't recognize him because of his new moustache and tan cap.

'What'd he die of?' he whispered to the tenant.

'I really couldn't say.'

But Mrs Panessa, walking behind the box, had heard.

'Old age,' she shrilly called back.

He tried to say some sweet thing but his tongue hung in his mouth like dead fruit on a tree, and his heart was a black-painted window.

Mrs Panessa moved away to live first with one stone-faced daughter, then with the other. And the bill was never paid.

The Last Mohican

Fidelman, a self-confessed failure as a painter, came to Italy to prepare a critical study of Giotto, the opening chapter of which he had carried across the ocean in a new pigskin leather brief-case, now gripped in his perspiring hand. Also new were his gum-soled oxblood shoes, a tweed suit he had on despite the late-September sun slanting hot in the Roman sky, although there was a lighter one in his bag; and a dacron shirt and set of cotton-dacron underwear, good for quick and easy washing for the traveller. His suit-case, a bulky, two-strapped affair which embarrassed him slightly, he had borrowed from his sister Bessie. He planned, if he had any money left at the end of the year, to buy a new one in Florence. Although he had been in not much of a mood when he had left the U.S.A., Fidelman picked up in Naples, and at the moment, as he stood in front of the Rome railroad station, after twenty minutes still absorbed in his first sight of the Eternal City, he was conscious of a certain exaltation that devolved on him after he had discovered that directly across the many-vehicled piazza stood the remains of the Baths of Diocletian. Fidelman remembered having read that Michelangelo had had a hand in converting the baths into a church and convent, the latter ultimately changed into the museum that presently was there. 'Imagine,' he muttered. 'Imagine all that history.'

In the midst of his imagining, Fidelman experienced the sensation of suddenly seeing himself as he was, to the pinpoint, outside and in, not without bittersweet pleasure; and as the well-known image of his face rose before him he was taken by the depth of pure feeling in his eyes, slightly magnified by glasses, and the sensitivity of his elongated nostrils and often tremulous lips, nose divided from lips by a moustache of recent vintage that looked, Fidelman thought, as if it had been sculptured there, adding to his dignified appearance although he was a little on the short side. But almost at the same moment, this unexpectedly intense sense of his being — it was more than appearance — faded, exaltation having gone where exaltation goes, and Fidelman became aware that there was an exterior source to the strange, almost tri-dimensional reflection of himself he had felt as well as seen. Behind him, a short distance to the right, he had noticed a stranger — give a skeleton a couple of pounds — loitering near a bronze statue on a stone pedestal of the heavy-dugged Etruscan wolf suckling the infant Romulus and Remus, the man contemplating Fidelman already acquisitively so as to suggest to the traveller that he had been mirrored (lock, stock, barrel) in the other's gaze for some time, perhaps since he had stepped off the train. Casually studying him, though pretending no, Fidelman beheld a person of about his own height, oddly dressed in brown knickers and black, knee-length woollen socks drawn up over slightly bowed, broomstick legs, these grounded in small, porous, pointed shoes. His yellowed shirt was open at the gaunt throat, both sleeves rolled up over skinny, hairy arms. The stranger's high forehead was bronzed, his black hair thick behind small ears, the dark, close-shaven beard tight on the face; his experienced nose was weighted at the tip, and the soft brown eyes, above all, *wanted*. Though his expression suggested humility, he all but licked his lips as he approached the ex-painter.

'Shalom,' he greeted Fidelman.

'Shalom,' the other hesitantly replied, uttering the word — so far as he recalled — for the first time in his life. My God, he thought, a handout for sure. My first hello in Rome and it has to be a schnorrer.

The stranger extended a smiling hand. 'Susskind,' he said, 'Shimon Susskind.'

'Arthur Fidelman.' Transferring his brief-case to under his left arm while standing astride the big suit-case, he shook hands with Susskind. A blue-smocked porter came by, glanced at Fidelman's bag, looked at him, then walked away.

Whether he knew it or not Susskind was rubbing his palms contemplatively together.

'Parla italiano?'

'Not with ease, although I read it fluently. You might say I need the practice.'

'Yiddish?'

'I express myself best in English.'

'Let it be English then.' Susskind spoke with a slight British intonation. 'I knew you were Jewish,' he said, 'the minute my eyes saw you.'

Fidelman chose to ignore the remark. 'Where did you pick up your knowledge of English?'

'In Israel.'

Israel interested Fidelman. 'You live there?'

'Once, not now,' Susskind answered vaguely. He seemed suddenly bored.

'How so?'

Susskind twitched a shoulder. 'Too much heavy labour for a man of my modest health. Also I couldn't stand the suspense.'

Fidelman nodded.

'Furthermore, the desert air makes me constipated. In Rome I am light hearted.'

'A Jewish refugee from Israel, no less,' Fidelman said good humouredly.

'I'm always running,' Susskind answered mirthlessly. If he was light hearted, he had yet to show it.

'Where else from, if I may ask?'

'Where else but Germany, Hungary, Poland? Where not?'

'Ah, that's so long ago.' Fidelman then noticed the grey in the man's hair. 'Well, I'd better be going,' he said. He picked up his bag as two porters hovered uncertainly near by.

But Susskind offered certain services. 'You got a hotel?'

'All picked and reserved.'

'How long are you staying?'

What business is it of his? However, Fidelman courteously replied, 'Two weeks in Rome, the rest of the year in Florence, with a few side trips to Siena, Assisi, Padua and maybe also Venice.'

'You wish a guide in Rome?'

'Are you a guide?'

'Why not?'

'No,' said Fidelman. 'I'll look as I go along to museums, libraries, et cetera.'

This caught Susskind's attention. 'What are you, a professor?'

Fidelman couldn't help blushing. 'Not exactly, really just a student.'

'From which institution?'

He coughed a little. 'By that I mean a professional student, you might say. Call me Trofimov, from Chekov. If there's something to learn I want to learn it.'

'You have some kind of a project?' the other persisted. 'A grant?'

'No grant. My money is hard earned. I worked and saved a long time to take a year in Italy. I made certain sacrifices. As for a project, I'm writing on the painter Giotto. He was one of the most important –'

'You don't have to tell me about Giotto,' Susskind interrupted with a little smile.

'You've studied his work?'

'Who doesn't know Giotto?'

'That's interesting to me,' said Fidelman, secretly irritated. 'How do you happen to know him?'

'How do you?'

'I've given a good deal of time and study to his work.'

'So I know him too.'

I'd better get this over with before it begins to amount up to something, Fidelman thought. He set down his bag and fished with a finger in his leather coin purse. The two porters watched with interest, one taking a sandwich out of his pocket, unwrapping the newspaper and beginning to eat.

'This is for yourself,' Fidelman said.

Susskind hardly glanced at the coin as he let it drop into his pants pocket. The porters then left.

The refugee had an odd way of standing motionless, like a cigar store Indian about to burst into flight. 'In your luggage,' he said vaguely, 'would you maybe have a suit you can't use? I could use a suit.'

At last he comes to the point. Fidelman, though annoyed, controlled himself. 'All I have is a change from the one you now see me wearing. Don't get the wrong idea about me, Mr Susskind. I'm not rich. In fact, I'm poor. Don't let a few new clothes deceive you. I owe my sister money for them.'

Susskind glanced down at his shabby, baggy knickers. 'I haven't had a suit for years. The one I was wearing when I ran away from Germany, fell apart. One day I was walking around naked.'

'Isn't there a welfare organization that could help you out – some group in the Jewish community, interested in refugees?'

'The Jewish organizations wish to give me what they wish, not what I wish,' Susskind replied bitterly. 'The only thing they offer me is a ticket back to Israel.'

'Why don't you take it?'

'I told you already, here I feel free.'

'Freedom is a relative term.'

'Don't tell me about freedom.'

He knows all about that, too, Fidelman thought. 'So you feel free,' he said, 'but how do you live?'

Susskind coughed, a brutal cough.

Fidelman was about to say something more on the subject of freedom but left it unsaid. Jesus, I'll be saddled with him all day if I don't watch out.

'I'd better be getting off to the hotel.' He bent again for his bag.

Susskind touched him on the shoulder and when Fidelman exasperatedly straightened up, the half dollar he had given the man was staring him in the eye.

'On this we both lose money.'

'How do you mean?'

'Today the lira sells six twenty-three on the dollar, but for specie they only give you five hundred.'

'In that case, give it here and I'll let you have a dollar.' From his billfold Fidelman quickly extracted a crisp bill and handed it to the refugee.

'Not more?' Susskind sighed.

'Not more,' the student answered emphatically.

'Maybe you would like to see Diocletian's bath? There are some enjoyable Roman coffins inside. I will guide you for another dollar.'

'No, thanks.' Fidelman said good-bye, and lifting the suit-case, lugged it to the kerb. A porter appeared and the student, after some hesitation, let him carry it towards the line of small dark-green taxis in the piazza. The porter offered to carry the brief-case too, but Fidelman wouldn't part with it. He gave the cab driver the address of the hotel, and the taxi took off with a lurch. Fidelman at last relaxed. Susskind, he noticed, had disappeared. Gone with his breeze, he thought. But on the way to the hotel he had an uneasy feeling that the refugee, crouched low, might be clinging to the little tyre on the back of the cab; however, he didn't look out to see.

Fidelman had reserved a room in an inexpensive hotel not far from the station, with its very convenient bus terminal. Then, as was his habit, he got himself quickly and tightly organized. He was always concerned with not wasting time, as if it were his only wealth – not true, of course, though Fidelman admitted he was an ambitious person – and he soon arranged a schedule that made the most of his working hours. Mornings he usually visited the Italian libraries, searching their catalogues and archives, read in poor light, and made profuse notes. He napped for an hour after lunch, then at four, when the churches and museums were re-opening, hurried off to them with lists of frescoes and paintings he must see. He was anxious to get to Florence, at the same time a little unhappy at all he would not have time to take in in

Rome. Fidelman promised himself to return again if he could afford it, perhaps in the spring, and look at anything he pleased.

After dark he managed to unwind himself and relax. He ate as the Romans did, late, enjoyed a half litre of white wine and smoked a cigarette. Afterward he liked to wander – especially in the old sections near the Tiber. He had read that here, under his feet, were the ruins of Ancient Rome. It was an inspiring business, he, Arthur Fidelman, after all, born a Bronx boy, walking around in all this history. History was mysterious, the remembrance of things unknown, in a way burdensome, in a way a sensuous experience. It uplifted and depressed, why he did not know, except that it excited his thoughts more than he thought good for him. This kind of excitement was all right up to a point, perfect maybe for a creative artist, but less so for a critic. A critic, he thought, should live on beans. He walked for miles along the winding river, gazing at the star-strewn skies. Once, after a couple of days in the Vatican Museum, he saw flights of angels – gold, blue, white – intermingled in the sky. 'My God, I got to stop using my eyes so much,' Fidelman said to himself. But back in his room he sometimes wrote till morning.

Late one night, about a week after his arrival in Rome, as Fidelman was writing notes on the Byzantine style mosaics he had seen during the day, there was a knock on the door, and though the student, immersed in his work, was not conscious he had said 'Avanti,' he must have, for the door opened, and instead of an angel, in came Susskind in his shirt and baggy knickers.

Fidelman, who had all but forgotten the refugee, certainly never thought of him, half rose in astonishment. 'Susskind,' he exclaimed, 'how did you get in here?'

Susskind for a moment stood motionless, then answered with a weary smile, 'I'll tell you the truth, I know the desk clerk.'

'But how did you know where I live?'

'I saw you walking in the street so I followed you.'

'You mean you saw me accidentally?'

'How else? Did you leave me your address?'

Fidelman resumed his seat. 'What can I do for you, Susskind?' He spoke grimly.

The refugee cleared his throat. 'Professor, the days are warm but the nights are cold. You see how I go around naked.' He held forth bluish arms, goosefleshed. 'I came to ask you to reconsider about giving away your old suit.'

'And who says it's an old suit?' Despite himself, Fidelman's voice thickened.

'One suit is new, so the other is old.'

'Not precisely. I am afraid I have no suit for you, Susskind. The one I presently have hanging in the closet is a little more than a year old and I can't afford to give it away. Besides, it's gabardine, more like a summer suit.'

'On me it will be for all seasons.'

After a moment's reflection, Fidelman drew out his billfold and counted four single dollars. These he handed to Susskind.

'Buy yourself a warm sweater.'

Susskind also counted the money. 'If four,' he said, 'then why not five?'

Fidelman flushed. The man's warped nerve. 'Because I happen to have four available,' he answered. 'That's twenty-five hundred lire. You should be able to buy a warm sweater and have something left over besides.'

'I need a suit,' Susskind said. 'The days are warm but the nights are cold.' He rubbed his arms. 'What else I need I won't say.'

'At least roll down your sleeves if you're so cold.'

'That won't help me.'

'Listen, Susskind,' Fidelman said gently, 'I would gladly give you the suit if I could afford to, but I can't. I have barely enough money to squeeze out a year for myself here. I've already told you I am indebted to my sister. Why don't you try to get yourself a job somewhere, no matter how menial? I'm sure that in a short while you'll work yourself up into a decent position.'

'A job, he says,' Susskind muttered gloomily. 'Do you

know what it means to get a job in Italy? Who will give me a job?'

'Who gives anybody a job? They have to go out and look for it.'

'You don't understand, professor. I am an Israeli citizen and this means I can only work for an Israeli company. How many Israeli companies are there here? – maybe two, El Al and Zim, and even if they had a job, they wouldn't give it to me because I have lost my passport. I would be better off now if I were stateless. A stateless person shows his laissez passer and sometimes he can find a small job.'

'But if you lost your passport why didn't you put in for a duplicate?'

'I did, but did they give it to me?'

'Why not?'

'Why not? They say I sold it.'

'Had they reason to think that?'

'I swear to you somebody stole it from me.'

'Under such circumstances,' Fidelman asked, 'how do you live?'

'How do I live?' He chomped with his teeth. 'I eat air.'

'Seriously?'

'Seriously, on air. I also peddle,' he confessed, 'but to peddle you need a licence, and that the Italians won't give me. When they caught me peddling I was interned for six months in a work camp.'

'Didn't they attempt to deport you?'

'They did, but I sold my mother's old wedding ring that I kept in my pocket so many years. The Italians are a humane people. They took the money and let me go but they told me not to peddle anymore.'

'So what do you do now?'

'I peddle. What should I do, beg? – I peddle. But last spring I got sick and gave my little money away to the doctors. I still have a bad cough.' He coughed fruitily. 'Now I have no capital to buy stock with. Listen, professor, maybe we can go in partnership together? Lend me twenty thousand lire and

I will buy ladies' nylon stockings. After I sell them I will return you your money.'

'I have no funds to invest, Susskind.'

'You will get it back, with interest.'

'I honestly am sorry for you,' Fidelman said, 'but why don't you at least do something practical? Why don't you go to the Joint Distribution Committee, for instance, and ask them to assist you? That's their business.'

'I already told you why. They wish me to go back, but I wish to stay here.'

'I still think going back would be the best thing for you.'

'No,' cried Susskind angrily.

'If that's your decision, freely made, then why pick on me? Am I responsible for you then, Susskind?'

'Who else?' Susskind loudly replied.

'Lower your voice, please, people are sleeping around here,' said Fidelman, beginning to perspire. 'Why should I be?'

'You know what responsibility means?'

'I think so.'

'Then you are responsible. Because you are a man. Because you are a Jew, aren't you?'

'Yes, goddamn it, but I'm not the only one in the whole wide world. Without prejudice, I refuse the obligation. I am a single individual and can't take on everybody's personal burden. I have the weight of my own to contend with.'

He reached for his billfold and plucked out another dollar.

'This makes five. It's more than I can afford, but take it and after this please leave me alone. I have made my contribution.'

Susskind stood there, oddly motionless, an impassioned statue, and for a moment Fidelman wondered if he would stay all night, but at last the refugee thrust forth a stiff arm, took the fifth dollar and departed.

Early the next morning Fidelman moved out of the hotel into another, less convenient for him, but far away from Shimon Susskind and his endless demands.

This was Tuesday. On Wednesday, after a busy morning in the library, Fidelman entered a nearby trattoria and ordered a plate of spaghetti with tomato sauce. He was reading his *Messaggero*, anticipating the coming of the food, for he was unusually hungry, when he sensed a presence at the table. He looked up, expecting the waiter, but beheld instead Susskind standing there, alas, unchanged.

Is there no escape from him? thought Fidelman, severely vexed. Is this why I came to Rome?

'Shalom, professor,' Susskind said, keeping his eyes off the table. 'I was passing and saw you sitting here alone, so I came in to say shalom.'

'Susskind,' Fidelman said in anger, 'have you been following me again?'

'How could I follow you?' asked the astonished Susskind. 'Do I know where you live now?'

Though Fidelman blushed a little, he told himself he owed nobody an explanation. So he had found out he had moved – good.

'My feet are tired. Can I sit five minutes?'

'Sit.'

Susskind drew out a chair. The spaghetti arrived, steaming hot. Fidelman sprinkled it with cheese and wound his fork into several tender strands. One of the strings of spaghetti seemed to stretch for miles, so he stopped at a certain point and swallowed the forkful. Having foolishly neglected to cut the long spaghetti string he was left sucking it, seemingly endlessly. This embarrassed him.

Susskind watched with rapt attention.

Fidelman at last reached the end of the long spaghetti, patted his mouth with a napkin, and paused in his eating.

'Would you care for a plateful?'

Susskind, eyes hungry, hesitated. 'Thanks,' he said.

'Thanks yes or thanks no?'

'Thanks no.' The eyes looked away.

Fidelman resumed eating, carefully winding his fork; he had had not too much practice with this sort of thing and was soon involved in the same dilemma with the spaghetti. Seeing Susskind still watching him, he soon became tense.

'We are not Italians, professor,' the refugee said. 'Cut it in small pieces with your knife. Then you will swallow it easier.'

'I'll handle it as I please,' Fidelman responded testily. 'This is my business. You attend to yours.'

'My business,' Susskind sighed, 'don't exist. This morning I had to let a wonderful chance get away from me. I had a chance to buy ladies' stockings at three hundred lire if I had money to buy half a gross. I could easily sell them for five hundred a pair. We would have made a nice profit.'

'The news doesn't interest me.'

'So if not ladies' stockings, I can also get sweaters, scarves, men's socks, also cheap leather goods, ceramics – whatever would interest you.'

'What interests me is what you did with the money I gave you for a sweater.'

'It's getting cold, professor,' Susskind said worriedly. 'Soon comes the November rains, and in winter the tramontana. I thought I ought to save your money to buy a couple of kilos of chestnuts and a bag of charcoal for my burner. If you sit all day on a busy street corner you can sometimes make a thousand lire. Italians like hot chestnuts. But if I do this I will need some warm clothes, maybe a suit.'

'A suit,' Fidelman remarked sarcastically, 'why not an overcoat?'

'I have a coat, poor that it is, but now I need a suit. How can anybody come in company without a suit?'

Fidelman's hand trembled as he laid down his fork. 'To my mind you are utterly irresponsible and I won't be saddled with you. I have the right to choose my own problems and the right to my privacy.'

'Don't get excited, professor, it's bad for your digestion. Eat in peace.' Susskind got up and left the trattoria.

Fidelman hadn't the appetite to finish his spaghetti. He paid the bill, waited ten minutes, then departed, glancing around

from time to time to see if he were being followed. He headed
down the sloping street to a small piazza where he saw
a couple of cabs. Not that he could afford one, but he wanted
to make sure Susskind didn't tail him back to his new hotel.
He would warn the clerk at the desk never to allow anybody
of the refugee's name or description even to make inquiries
about him.

Susskind, however, stepped out from behind a plashing
fountain at the centre of the little piazza. Modestly addres-
sing the speechless Fidelman, he said, 'I don't wish to take
only, professor. If I had something to give you, I would give
it to you.'

'Thanks,' snapped Fidelman, 'just give me some peace of
mind.'

'That you have to find yourself,' Susskind answered.

In the taxi Fidelman decided to leave for Florence the next
day, rather than at the end of the week, and once and for all
be done with the pest.

That night, after returning to his room from an unpleasur-
able walk in the Trastevere – he had a headache from too much
wine at supper – Fidelman found his door ajar and at once
recalled that he had forgotten to lock it, although he had as
usual left the key with the desk clerk. He was at first frightened, but when he tried the armadio in which he kept
his clothes and suit-case, it was shut tight. Hastily unlocking
it, he was relieved to see his blue gabardine suit – a one-but-
ton jacket affair, the trousers a little frayed on the cuffs, but
all in good shape and usable for years to come – hanging
amid some shirts the maid had pressed for him; and when he
examined the contents of the suitcase he found nothing missing, including, thank God, his passport and travellers'
cheques. Gazing around the room, Fidelman saw all in place.
Satisfied, he picked up a book and read ten pages before he
thought of his brief-case. He jumped to his feet and began to
search everywhere, remembering distinctly that it had been
on the night table as he had laid on the bed that afternoon,
re-reading his chapter. He searched under the bed and behind

the night table, then again throughout the room, even on top of and behind the armadio. Fidelman hopelessly opened every drawer, no matter how small, but found neither the brief-case, nor, what was worse, the chapter in it.

With a groan he sank down on the bed, insulting himself for not having made a copy of the manuscript, for he had more than once warned himself that something like this might happen to it. But he hadn't because there were some revisions he had contemplated making, and he had planned to retype the entire chapter before beginning the next. He thought now of complaining to the owner of the hotel, who lived on the floor below, but it was already past midnight and he realized nothing could be done until morning. Who could have taken it? The maid or hall porter? It seemed unlikely they would risk their jobs to steal a piece of leather goods that would bring them only a few thousand lire in a pawn shop. Possibly a sneak thief? He would ask tomorrow if other persons on the floor were missing something. He somehow doubted it. If a thief, he would then and there have ditched the chapter and stuffed the brief case with Fidelman's oxblood shoes, left by the bed, and the fifteen-dollar R. A. Macy sweater that lay in full view of the desk. But if not the maid or porter or a sneak thief, then who? Though Fidelman had not the slightest shred of evidence to support his suspicions he could think of only one person – Susskind. This thought stung him. But if Susskind, why? Out of pique, perhaps, that he had not been given the suit he had coveted, nor was able to pry it out of the armadio? Try as he would, Fidelman could think of no one else and no other reason. Somehow the pedlar had followed him home (he suspected their meeting at the fountain) and had got into his room while he was out to supper.

Fidelman's sleep that night was wretched. He dreamed of pursuing the refugee in the Jewish catacombs under the ancient Appian Way, threatening him a blow on the presumptuous head with a seven-flamed candelabrum he clutched in his hand; while Susskind, clever ghost, who knew the ins and outs of all the crypts and alleys, eluded him at every turn.

Then Fidelman's candles all blew out, leaving him sightless
and alone in the cemeterial dark; but when the student arose
in the morning and wearily drew up the blinds, the yellow
Italian sun winked him cheerfully in both bleary eyes.

Fidelman postponed going to Florence. He reported his loss
to the Questura, and though the police were polite and eager
to help, they could do nothing for him. On the form on which
the inspector noted the complaint, he listed the brief-case as
worth ten thousand lire, and for 'valor del manuscritto' he
drew a line. Fidelman, after giving the matter a good deal of
thought, did not report Susskind, first, because he had absolutely no proof, for the desk clerk swore he had seen no
stranger around in knickers; second, because he was afraid of
the consequences for the refugee if he were written down
'suspected thief' as well as 'unlicensed pedlar' and inveter-
ate refugee. He tried instead to rewrite the chapter, which he
felt sure he knew by heart, but when he sat down at the desk,
there were important thoughts, whole paragraphs, even pages,
that went blank in the mind. He considered sending to
America for his notes for the chapter but they were in a barrel in his sister's attic in Levittown, among many notes for
other projects. The thought of Bessie, a mother of five, poking
around in his things, and the work entailed in sorting the
cards, then getting them packaged and mailed to him across
the ocean, wearied Fidelman unspeakably; he was certain she
would send the wrong ones. He laid down his pen and went
into the street, seeking Susskind. He searched for him in
neighbourhoods where he had seen him before, and though
Fidelman spent hours looking, literally days, Susskind never
appeared; or if he perhaps did, the sight of Fidelman caused
him to vanish. And when the student inquired about him at
the Israeli consulate, the clerk, a new man on the job, said he
had no record of such a person or his lost passport; on the other
hand, he was known at the Joint Distribution Committee,
but by name and address only, an impossibility, Fidelman
thought. They gave him a number to go to but the place had

long since been torn down to make way for an apartment house.

Time went without work, without accomplishment. To put an end to this appalling waste Fidelman tried to force himself back into his routine of research and picture viewing. He moved out of the hotel, which he now could not stand for the harm it had done him (leaving a telephone number and urging he be called if the slightest clue turned up), and he took a room in a small pensione near the Stazione and here had breakfast and supper rather than go out. He was much concerned with expenditures and carefully recorded them in a notebook he had acquired for the purpose. Nights, instead of wandering in the city, feasting himself upon its beauty and mystery, he kept his eyes glued to paper, sitting stead-fastly at his desk in an attempt to recreate his initial chapter, because he was lost without a beginning. He had tried writing the second chapter from notes in his possession but it had come to nothing. Always Fidelman needed something solid behind him before he could advance, some worthwhile accomplishment upon which to build another. He worked late, but his mood, or inspiration, or whatever it was, had deserted him, leaving him with growing anxiety, almost disorientation; of not knowing – it seemed to him for the first time in months – what he must do next, a feeling that was torture. Therefore he again took up his search for the refugee. He thought now that once he had settled it, knew that the man had or hadn't stolen his chapter – whether he recovered it or not seemed at the moment immaterial – just the knowing of it would ease his mind and again he would *feel* like working, the crucial element.

Daily he combed the crowded streets, searching for Suss-kind wherever people peddled. On successive Sunday mornings he took the long ride to the Porta Portese market and hunted for hours among the piles of second-hand goods and junk lining the back streets, hoping his brief case would magi-cally appear, though it never did. He visited the open market at Piazza Fontanella Borghese, and observed the ambulant

vendors at Piazza Dante. He looked among fruit and vege-
table stalls set up in the streets, whenever he chanced upon
them, and dawdled on busy street corners after dark, among
beggars and fly-by-night pedlars. After the first cold snap at
the end of October, when the chestnut sellers appeared
throughout the city, huddled over pails of glowing coals, he
sought in their faces the missing Susskind. Where in all of
modern and ancient Rome was he? The man lived in the open
air – he had to appear somewhere. Sometimes when riding in
a bus or tram, Fidelman thought he had glimpsed somebody
in a crowd, dressed in the refugee's clothes, and he invariably
got off to run after whoever it was – once a man standing in
front of the Banco di Santo Spirito, gone when Fidelman
breathlessly arrived; and another time he overtook a person in
knickers, but this one wore a monocle. Sir Ian Susskind?

In November it rained. Fidelman wore a blue beret with his
trench coat and a pair of black Italian shoes, smaller, despite
their pointed toes, than his burly oxbloods which overheated
his feet and whose colour he detested. But instead of visiting
museums he frequented movie houses sitting in the cheapest
seats and regretting the cost. He was, at odd hours in certain
streets, several times accosted by prostitutes, some heart-
breakingly pretty, one a slender, unhappy-looking girl with
bags under her eyes whom he desired mightily, but Fidelman
feared for his health. He had got to know the face of Rome
and spoke Italian fairly fluently, but his heart was burdened,
and in his blood raged a murderous hatred of the bandy-legged
refugee – although there were times when he bethought himself he might be wrong – so Fidelman more than once cursed
him to perdition.

One Friday night, as the first star glowed over the Tiber,
Fidelman, walking aimlessly along the left riverbank, came
upon a synagogue and wandered in among a crowd of Sephardim with Italianate faces. One by one they paused before a
sink in an antechamber to dip their hands under a flowing
faucet, then in the house of worship touched with loose

fingers their brows, mouths, and breasts as they bowed to the Arc, Fidelman doing likewise. Where in the world am I? Three rabbis rose from a bench and the service began, a long prayer, sometimes chanted, sometimes accompanied by invisible organ music, but no Susskind anywhere. Fidelman sat at a desk-like pew in the last row, where he could inspect the congregants yet keep an eye on the door. The synagogue was unheated and the cold rose like an exudation from the marble floor. The student's freezing nose burned like a lit candle. He got up to go, but the beadle, a stout man in a high hat and short caftan, wearing a long thick silver chain around his neck, fixed the student with his powerful left eye.

'From New York?' he inquired, slowly approaching.

Half the congregation turned to see who.

'State, not city,' answered Fidelman, nursing an active guilt for the attention he was attracting. Then, taking advantage of a pause, he whispered, 'Do you happen to know a man named Susskind? He wears knickers.'

'A relative?' The beadle gazed at him sadly.

'Not exactly.'

'My own son – killed in the Ardeatine Caves.' Tears stood forth in his eyes.

'Ah, for that I'm sorry.'

But the beadle had exhausted the subject. He wiped his wet lids with pudgy fingers and the curious Sephardim turned back to their prayer books.

'Which Susskind?' the beadle wanted to know.

'Shimon.'

He scratched his ear. 'Look in the ghetto.'

'I looked.'

'Look again.'

The beadle walked slowly away and Fidelman sneaked out.

The ghetto lay behind the synagogue for several crooked, well-packed blocks, encompassing aristocratic palazzi ruined by age and unbearable numbers, their discoloured façades strung with lines of withered wet wash, the fountains in the piazzas, dirt-laden, dry. And dark stone tenements, built partly on centuries-old ghetto walls, inclined towards one another across narrow, cobblestoned streets. In and among the impoverished houses were the wholesale establishments of wealthy Jews, dark holes ending in jewelled interiors, silks and silver of all colours. In the mazed streets wandered the present-day poor, Fidelman among them, oppressed by history, although, he joked to himself, it added years to his life.

A white moon shone upon the ghetto, lighting it like dark day. Once he thought he saw a ghost he knew by sight, and hastily followed him through a thick stone passage to a blank wall where shone in white letters under a tiny electric bulb: VIETATO URINARE. Here was a smell but no Susskind.

For thirty lire the student bought a dwarfed, blackened banana from a street vendor (not S) on a bicycle, and stopped to eat. A crowd of ragazzi gathered to watch.

'Anybody here know Susskind, a refugee wearing knickers?' Fidelman announced, stooping to point with the banana where the pants went beneath the knees. He also made his legs a trifle bowed but nobody noticed.

There was no response until he had finished his fruit, then a thin-faced boy with brown liquescent eyes out of Murillo, piped: 'He sometimes works in the Cimitero Verano, the Jewish section.'

There too? thought Fidelman. 'Works in the cemetery?' he inquired. 'With a shovel?'

'He prays for the dead,' the boy answered, 'for a small fee.'

Fidelman bought him a quick banana and the others dispersed.

In the cemetery, deserted on the Sabbath – he should have come Sunday – Fidelman went among the graves, reading legends carved on tombstones, many topped with small brass candelabra, whilst withered yellow chrysanthemums lay on the stone tablets of other graves, dropped stealthily, Fidelman imagined, on All Souls Day – a festival in another part of the cemetery – by renegade sons and daughters unable to bear the sight of their dead bereft of flowers, while the crypts of the goyim were lit and in bloom. Many were burial places,

he read on the stained stones, of those who, for one reason or
another, had died in the late large war, including an empty
place, it said under a six-pointed star engraved upon a marble
slab that lay on the ground, for 'My beloved father/ Betrayed
by the damned Fascists/Murdered at Auschwitz by the bar-
barous Nazis/ *O Crime Orribile.*' But no Susskind.

Three months had gone by since Fidelman's arrival in Rome.
Should he, he many times asked himself, leave the city and
this foolish search? Why not off to Florence, and there, amid
the art splendours of the world, be inspired to resume his
work? But the loss of his first chapter was like a spell cast over
him. There were times he scorned it as a man-made thing, like
all such, replaceable; other times he feared it was not the chapter per se, but that his volatile curiosity had become somehow
entangled with Susskind's strange personality – Had he repaid generosity by stealing a man's life work? Was he so distorted? To satisfy himself, to know man, Fidelman had to
know, though at what a cost in precious time and effort. Sometimes he smiled wryly at all this; ridiculous, the chapter
grieved him for itself only – the precious thing he had created
then lost – especially when he got to thinking of the long dili-
gent labour, how painstakingly he had built each idea, how
cleverly mastered problems of order, form, how impressive the
finished product, Giotto reborn ! It broke the heart. What else,
if after months he was here, still seeking?
And Fidelman was unchangingly convinced that Susskind
had taken it, or why would he still be hiding? He sighed much
and gained weight. Mulling over his frustrated career, on the
backs of envelopes containing unanswered letters from his sister Bessie he aimlessly sketched little angels flying. Once,
studying his minuscule drawings, it occurred to him that he
might someday return to painting, but the thought was more
painful than Fidelman could bear.
One bright morning in mid-December, after a good night's
sleep, his first in weeks, he vowed he would have another look
at the Navicella and then be off to Florence. Shortly before

noon he visited the porch of St Peter's, trying, from his remembrance of Giotto's sketch, to see the mosaic as it had been
before its many restorations. He hazarded a note or two in
shaky handwriting, then left the church and was walking
down the sweeping flight of stairs, when he beheld at the bottom – his heart misgave him, was he still seeing pictures, a
sneaky apostle added to the overloaded boatful? – ecco, Susskind! The refugee, in beret and long green G.I. raincoat, from
under whose skirts showed his black-stockinged, rooster's ankles – indicating knickers going on above though hidden –
was selling black and white rosaries to all who would buy. He
held several strands of beads in one hand, while in the palm
of the other a few gilded medallions glinted in the winter sun.
Despite his outer clothing, Susskind looked, it must be said,
unchanged, not a pound more of meat or muscle, the face
though aged, ageless. Gazing at him, the student ground his
teeth in remembrance. He was tempted quickly to hide, and
unobserved observe the thief; but his impatience, after the
long unhappy search, was too much for him. With controlled trepidation he approached Susskind on his left as the refugee was busily engaged on the right, urging a sale of beads
upon a woman drenched in black.

'Beads, rosaries, say your prayers with holy beads.'

'Greetings, Susskind,' Fidelman said, coming shakily down
the stairs, dissembling the Unified Man, all peace and con-
tentment. 'One looks for you everywhere and finds you here.
Wie gehts?'

Susskind, though his eyes flickered, showed no surprise to
speak of. For a moment his expression seemed to say he had
no idea who was this, had forgotten Fidelman's existence, but
then at last remembered – somebody long ago from another
country, whom you smiled on, then forgot.

'Still here?' he perhaps ironically joked.

'Still,' Fidelman was embarrassed at his voice slipping.

'Rome holds you?'

'Rome,' faltered Fidelman, '– the air.' He breathed deep and
exhaled with emotion.

Noticing the refugee was not truly attentive, his eyes roving upon potential customers, Fidelman, girding himself, remarked, 'By the way, Susskind, you didn't happen to notice – did you? – the brief-case I was carrying with me around the time we met in September?'

'Brief-case – what kind?' This he said absently, his eyes on the church doors.

'Pigskin. I had in it –' Here Fidelman's voice could be heard cracking, '– a chapter of a critical work on Giotto I was writing. You know, I'm sure, the Trecento painter?'

'Who doesn't know Giotto?'

'Do you happen to recall whether you saw, if, that is –' He stopped, at a loss for words other than accusatory.

'Excuse me – business.' Susskind broke away and bounced up the steps two at a time. A man he approached shied away. He had beads, didn't need others.

Fidelman had followed the refugee. 'Reward,' he muttered up close to his ear. 'Fifteen thousand for the chapter, and who has it can keep the brand new brief-case. That's his business, no questions asked. Fair enough?'

Susskind spied a lady tourist, including camera and guide book. 'Beads – holy beads.' He held up both hands, but she was just a Lutheran, passing through.

'Slow today,' Susskind complained as they walked down the stairs, 'but maybe it's the items. Everybody has the same. If I had some big ceramics of the Holy Mother, they go like hot cakes – a good investment for somebody with a little cash.'

'Use the reward for that,' Fidelman cagily whispered, 'buy Holy Mothers.'

If he heard, Susskind gave no sign. At the sight of a family of nine emerging from the main portal above, the refugee, calling addio over his shoulder, fairly flew up the steps. But Fidelman uttered no response. I'll get the rat yet. He went off to hide behind a high fountain in the square. But the flying spume raised by the wind wet him, so he retreated behind a massive column and peeked out at short intervals to keep the pedlar in sight.

At two o'clock, when St Peter's closed to visitors, Susskind dumped his goods into his raincoat pockets and locked up shop. Fidelman followed him all the way home, indeed the ghetto, although along a street he had not consciously been on before, which led into an alley where the refugee pulled open a left-handed door, and without transition, was 'home'. Fidelman, sneaking up close, caught a dim glimpse of an overgrown closet containing bed and table. He found no address on wall or door, nor, to his surprise, any door lock. This for a moment depressed him. It meant Susskind had nothing worth stealing. Of his own, that is. The student promised himself to return tomorrow, when the occupant was elsewhere.

Return he did, in the morning, while the entrepreneur was out selling religious articles, glanced around once and was quickly inside. He shivered – a pitch black freezing cave. Fidelman scratched up a thick match and confirmed bed and table, also a rickety chair, but no heat or light except a drippy candle stub in a saucer on the table. He lit the yellow candle and searched all over the place. In the table drawer a few eating implements plus safety razor, though where he shaved was a mystery, probably a public toilet. On a shelf above the thin-blanketed bed stood half a flask of red wine, part of a package of spaghetti, and a hard panino. Also an unexpected little fish bowl with a bony gold fish swimming around in Arctic seas. The fish, reflecting the candle flame, gulped repeatedly, threshing its frigid tail as Fidelman watched. He loves pets, thought the student. Under the bed he found a chamber pot, but nowhere a brief-case with a fine critical chapter in it. The place was not more than an ice-box someone probably had lent the refugee to come in out of the rain. Alas, Fidelman sighed. Back in the pensione, it took a hot water bottle two hours to thaw him out; but from the visit he never fully recovered.

In this latest dream of Fidelman's he was spending the day in a cemetery all crowded with tombstones, when up out of an empty grave rose this long-nosed brown shade, Virgilio Susskind, beckoning.

Fidelman hurried over.

'Have you read Tolstoy?'

'Sparingly.'

'Why is art?' asked the shade, drifting off.

Fidelman, willy nilly, followed, and the ghost, as it vanished, led him up steps going through the ghetto and into a marble synagogue.

The student, left alone, for no reason he could think of lay down upon the stone floor, his shoulders keeping strangely warm as he stared at the sunlit vault above. The fresco therein revealed this saint in fading blue, the sky flowing from his head, handing an old knight in a thin red robe his gold cloak. Nearby stood a humble horse and two stone hills.

Giotto. San Francesco dona le vesti al cavaliere povero.

Fidelman awoke running. He stuffed his blue gabardine into a paper bag, caught a bus, and knocked early on Susskind's heavy portal.

'Avanti.' The refugee, already garbed in beret and raincoat (probably his pyjamas), was standing at the table, lighting the candle with a flaming sheet of paper. To Fidelman the paper looked the underside of a typewritten page. Despite himself, the student recalled in letters of fire his entire chapter.

'Here, Susskind,' he said in a trembling voice, offering the bundle, 'I bring you my suit. Wear it in good health.'

The refugee glanced at it without expression. 'What do you wish for it?'

'Nothing at all.' Fidelman laid the bag on the table, called good-bye and left.

He soon heard footsteps clattering after him across the cobblestones.

'Excuse me, I kept this under my mattress for you.' Susskind thrust at him the pigskin brief-case.

Fidelman savagely opened it, searching frenziedly in each compartment, but the bag was empty. The refugee was already in flight. With a bellow the student started after him. 'You bastard, you burned my chapter!'

'Have mercy,' cried Susskind, 'I did you a favour.'

'I'll do you one and cut your throat.'

The words were there but the spirit was missing.

In a towering rage, Fidelman forced a burst of speed, but the refugee, light as the wind in his marvellous knickers, his green coattails flying, rapidly gained ground.

The ghetto Jews, framed in amazement in their medieval windows, stared at the wild pursuit. But in the middle of it, Fidelman, stout and short of breath, moved by all he had lately learned, had a triumphant insight.

'Susskind, come back,' he shouted, half sobbing. 'The suit is yours. All is forgiven.'

He came to a dead halt but the refugee ran on. When last seen he was still running.

The Loan

The sweet, the heady smell of Lieb's white bread drew customers in droves long before the loaves were baked. Alert behind the counter, Bessie, Lieb's second wife, discerned a stranger among them, a frail, gnarled man with a hard hat who hung, disjoined, at the edge of the crowd. Though the stranger looked harmless enough among the aggressive purchasers of baked goods, she was at once concerned. Her glance questioned him but he signalled with a deprecatory nod of his hatted head that he would wait – glad to (forever) – though his face glittered with misery. If suffering had marked him, he no longer sought to conceal the sign; the shining was his own – him – now. So he frightened Bessie.

She made quick hash of the customers, and when they, after her annihilating service, were gone, she returned him her stare.

He tipped his hat. 'Pardon me – Kobotsky. Is Lieb the baker here?'

'Who Kobotsky?'

'An old friend' – frightening her further.

'From where?'

'From long ago.'

'What do you want to see him?'

The question insulted, so Kobotsky was reluctant to say.

As if drawn into the shop by the magic of a voice, the baker, shirtless, appeared from the rear. His pink, fleshy arms had been deep in dough. For a hat he wore jauntily a flour-covered brown paper sack. His peering glasses were dusty with flour, and the inquisitive face white with it so that he resembled a paunchy ghost; but the ghost, through the glasses, was Kobotsky, not he.

'Kobotsky,' the baker cried almost with a sob, for it was so many years gone Kobotsky reminded him of, when they were both at least young, and circumstances were – ah, different. Unable, for sentimental reasons, to refrain from smarting tears, he jabbed them away with a thrust of the hand.

Kobotsky removed his hat – he had grown all but bald where Lieb was grey – and patted his flushed forehead with an immaculate handkerchief.

Lieb sprang forward with a stool. 'Sit, Kobotsky.'

'Not here,' Bessie murmured.

'Customers,' she explained to Kobotsky. 'Soon comes the supper rush.'

'Better in the back,' nodded Kobotsky.

So that was where they went, happier for the privacy. But it happened that no customers came so Bessie went in to hear.

Kobotsky sat enthroned on a tall stool in a corner of the room, stoop-shouldered, his black coat and hat on, the stiff, grey-veined hands drooping over thin thighs. Lieb, peering through full moons, eased his bones on a flour sack. Bessie lent an attentive ear, but the visitor was dumb. Embarrassed, Lieb did the talking: ah, of old times. The world was new. We were, Kobotsky, young. Do you remember how both together, immigrants out of steerage, we registered in night school?

'Haben, hatte, gehabt.' He cackled at the sound of it.

No word from the gaunt one on the stool. Bessie fluttered around an impatient duster. She shot a glance into the shop: empty.

Lieb, acting the life of the party, recited, to cheer his friend: ' "Come," said the wind to the trees one day, "Come over the meadow with me and play." Remember, Kobotsky?'

Bessie sniffed aloud. 'Lieb, the bread!'

The baker bounced up, strode over to the gas oven and pulled one of the tiered doors down. Just in time he yanked out the trays of brown breads in hot pans, and set them on the tin-top worktable.

Bessie clucked at the narrow escape.

Lieb peered into the shop. 'Customers,' he said triumphantly. Flushed, she went in. Kobotsky, with wetted lips, watched her go. Lieb set to work moulding the risen dough in a bowl into two trays of pans. Soon the bread was baking, but Bessie was back.

The honey odour of the new loaves distracted Kobotsky. He breathed the sweet fragrance as if this were the first air he was tasting, and even beat his fist against his chest at the delicious smell.

'Oh, my God,' he all but wept. 'Wonderful.'

'With tears,' Lieb said humbly, pointing to the large pot of dough.

Kobotsky nodded.

For thirty years, the baker explained, he was never with a penny to his name. One day, out of misery, he had wept into the dough. Thereafter his bread was such it brought customers in from everywhere.

'My cakes they don't like so much, but my bread and rolls they run miles to buy.'

Kobotsky blew his nose, then peeked into the shop: three customers.

'Lieb' – a whisper.

Despite himself the baker stiffened.

The visitor's eyes swept back to Bessie out front, then, under raised brows, questioned the baker.

Lieb, however, remained mute.

Kobotsky coughed clear his throat. 'Lieb, I need two hundred dollars.' His voice broke.

Lieb slowly sank onto the sack. He knew – had known. From the minute of Kobotsky's appearance he had weighed in his thoughts the possibility of this against the remembrance of the lost and bitter hundred, fifteen years ago. Kobotsky swore he had repaid it, Lieb said no. Afterwards a broken friendship. It took years to blot out of the system the memoried outrage.

Kobotsky bowed his head.

At least admit you were wrong, Lieb thought, waiting a cruelly long time.

Kobotsky stared at his crippled hands. Once a cutter of furs, driven by arthritis out of the business.

Lieb gazed too. The button of a truss bit into his belly. Both eyes were cloudy with cataracts. Though the doctor swore he would see after the operation, he feared otherwise.

He sighed. The wrong was in the past. Forgiven: forgiven at the dim sight of him.

'For myself, positively, but she' – Lieb nodded towards the shop – 'is a second wife. Everything is in her name.' He held up empty hands.

Kobotsky's eyes were shut.

'But I will ask her –' Lieb looked doubtful.

'My wife needs –'

The baker raised a palm. 'Don't speak.'

'Tell her –'

'Leave it to me.'

He seized the broom and circled the room, raising clouds of white dust.

When Bessie, breathless, got back she threw one look at them, and with tightened lips, waited adamant.

Lieb hastily scoured the pots in the iron sink, stored the bread pans under the table and stacked the fragrant loaves. He put one eye to the slot of the oven: baking, all baking.

Facing Bessie, he broke into a sweat so hot it momentarily stunned him.

Kobotsky squirmed atop the stool.

'Bessie,' said the baker at last, 'this is my old friend.'

She nodded gravely.

Kobotsky lifted his hat.

'His mother – God bless her – gave me many times a plate hot soup. Also when I came to this country, for years I ate at his table. His wife is a very fine person – Dora – you will some-day meet her –'

Kobotsky softly groaned.

'So why I didn't meet her yet?' Bessie said, after a dozen years, still jealous of the first wife's prerogatives.

'You will.'

'Why didn't I?'

'Lieb –' pleaded Kobotsky.

'Because I didn't see her myself fifteen years,' Lieb admitted.

'Why not?' she pounced.

Lieb paused. 'A mistake.'

Kobotsky turned away.

'My fault,' said Lieb.

'Because you never go any place,' Bessie spat out. 'Because you live always in the shop. Because it means nothing to you to have friends.'

Lieb solemnly agreed.

'Now she is sick,' he announced. 'The doctor must operate. This will cost two hundred dollars. I promised Kobotsky –'

Bessie screamed.

Hat in hand, Kobotsky got off the stool.

Pressing a palm to her bosom, Bessie lifted her arm to her eyes. She tottered. They both ran forward to catch her but she did not fall. Kobotsky retreated quickly to the stool and Lieb returned to the sink.

Bessie, her face like the inside of a loaf, quietly addressed the visitor. 'I have pity for your wife but we can't help you. I am sorry, Mr Kobotsky, we are poor people, we don't have the money.'

'A mistake,' Lieb cried, enraged.

Bessie strode over to the shelf and tore out a bill box. She dumped its contents on the table, the papers flying everywhere.

'Bills,' she shouted.

Kobotsky hunched his shoulders.

'Bessie, we have in the bank –'

'No –'

'I saw the bankbook.'

'So what if you saved a few dollars, so have you got life insurance?'

He made no answer.

'Can you get?' she taunted.

The front door banged. It banged often. The shop was crowded with customers clamouring for bread. Bessie stomped out to wait on them.

In the rear the wounded stirred. Kobotsky, with bony fingers buttoned his overcoat.

'Sit,' sighed the baker.

'Lieb, I am sorry –'

Kobotsky sat, his face lit with sadness.

When Bessie finally was rid of the rush, Lieb went into the shop. He spoke to her quietly, almost in a whisper, and she answered as quietly, but it took only a minute to start them quarrelling.

Kobotsky slipped off the stool. He went to the sink, wet half his handkerchief, he thrust it into his overcoat pocket, then took out a small penknife and quickly pared his fingernails.

As he entered the shop, Lieb was pleading with Bessie, reciting the embittered hours of his toil, the enduring drudgery. And now that he had a cent to his name, what was there to live for if he could not share it with a dear friend? But Bessie had her back to him.

'Please,' Kobotsky said, 'don't fight. I will go away now.'

Lieb gazed at him in exasperation, Bessie stayed with head averted.

'Yes,' Kobotsky sighed, 'the money I wanted for Dora, but she is not sick, Lieb, she is dead.'

'Ai,' Lieb cried, wringing his hands.

Bessie faced the visitor, pallid.

'Not now,' he spoke kindly, 'five years ago.'

Lieb groaned.

'The money I need for a stone on her grave. She never had a stone. Next Sunday is five years that she is dead and every year I promise her, "Dora, this year I will give you your stone," and every year I gave her nothing.'

The grave, to his everlasting shame, lay uncovered before all eyes. He had long ago paid a fifty-dollar deposit for a headstone with her name on it in clearly chiselled letters, but had never got the rest of the money. If there wasn't one thing to do with it there was always another: first an operation; the second year he couldn't work, imprisoned again by arthritis; the third a widowed sister lost her only son and the little Kobotsky earned had to help support her; the fourth incapacitated by boils that made him ashamed to walk out into the street. This year he was at least working, but only for just enough to eat and sleep, so Dora still lay without a stone, and for aught he knew he would some day return to the cemetery and find her grave gone.

Tears sprang into the baker's eyes. One gaze at Bessie's face – at the odd looseness of neck and shoulders – told him that she too was moved. Ah, he had won out. She would now say yes, give the money, and they would then all sit down at the table and eat together.

But Bessie, though weeping, shook her head, and before they could guess what, had blurted out the story of her afflictions: how the Bolsheviki came when she was a little girl and dragged her beloved father into the snowy fields without his shoes; the shots scattered the blackbirds in the trees and the snow oozed blood; how, when she was married a year, her husband, a sweet and gentle man, an educated accountant – rare in those days and that place – died of typhus in Warsaw; and how she, abandoned in her grief, years later found sanctuary in the home of an older brother in Germany, who sacrificed his own chances to send her, before the war, to America, and himself ended, with wife and daughter, in one of Hitler's incinerators.

'So I came to America and met here a poor baker, a poor man – who was always in his life poor – without a penny and without enjoyment in his life, and I married him, God knows why, and with my both hands, working day and night, I fixed up for him his piece of business and we make now, after twelve years, a little living. But Lieb is not a healthy man, also with eyes that he needs an operation, and this is not yet everything. Suppose, God forbid, that he died, what will I do alone by myself? Where will I go, where, and who will take care of me if I have nothing?'

The baker, who had often heard this tale, munched, as he listened, chunks of white bread.

When she had finished he tossed the shell of a loaf away. Kobotsky, at the end of the story, held his hands over his ears.

Tears streaming from her eyes, Bessie raised her head and suspiciously sniffed the air. Screeching suddenly, she ran into the rear and with a cry wrenched open the oven door. A cloud of smoke billowed out at her. The loaves in the trays were blackened bricks – charred corpses.

Kobotsky and the baker embraced and sighed over their lost youth. They pressed mouths together and parted forever.

The Magic Barrel

Not long ago there lived in uptown New York, in a small, almost meagre room, though crowded with books, Leo Finkle, a rabbinical student in the Yeshivah University. Finkle, after six years of study, was to be ordained in June and had been advised by an acquaintance that he might find it easier to win himself a congregation if he were married. Since he had no present prospects of marriage, after two tormented days of turning it over in his mind, he called in Pinye Salzman, a marriage broker whose two-line advertisement he had read in the *Forward*.

The matchmaker appeared one night out of the dark fourth-floor hallway of the greystone rooming house where Finkle lived, grasping a black, strapped portfolio that had been worn thin with use. Salzman, who had been long in the business, was of slight but dignified build, wearing an old hat, and an overcoat too short and tight for him. He smelled frankly of fish, which he loved to eat, and although he was missing a few teeth, his presence was not displeasing, because of an amiable manner curiously contrasted with mournful eyes. His voice, his lips, his wisp of beard, his bony fingers were animated, but give him a moment of repose and his mild blue eyes revealed a depth of sadness, a characteristic that put Leo a little at ease although the situation, for him, was inherently tense.

He at once informed Salzman why he had asked him to come, explaining that his home was in Cleveland, and that but for his parents, who had married comparatively late in life, he was alone in the world. He had for six years devoted himself almost entirely to his studies, as a result of which, understandably, he had found himself without time for a social life and the company of young women. Therefore he thought it the better part of trial and error – of embarrassing fumbling – to call in an experienced person to advise him on these matters. He remarked in passing that the function of the marriage broker was ancient and honourable, highly approved in the Jewish community, because it made practical the necessary without hindering joy. Moreover, his own parents had been brought together by a matchmaker. They had made, if not a financially profitable marriage – since neither had possessed any worldly goods to speak of – at least a successful one in the sense of their everlasting devotion to each other. Salzman listened in embarrassed surprise, sensing a sort of apology. Later, however, he experienced a glow of pride in his work, an emotion that had left him years ago, and he heartily approved of Finkle.

The two went to their business. Leo had led Salzman to the only clear place in the room, a table near a window that overlooked the lamp-lit city. He seated himself at the matchmaker's side but facing him, attempting by an act of will to suppress the unpleasant tickle in his throat. Salzman eagerly unstrapped his portfolio and removed a loose rubber band from a thin packet of much-handled cards. As he flipped through them, a gesture and sound that physically hurt Leo, the student pretended not to see and gazed steadfastly out the window. Although it was still February, winter was on its last legs, signs of which he had for the first time in years begun to notice. He now observed the round white moon, moving high in the sky through a cloud menagerie, and watched with half-open mouth as it penetrated a huge hen, and dropped out of her like an egg laying itself. Salzman, though pretending through eyeglasses he had just slipped on, to be engaged in scanning the writing on the cards, stole occasional glances at the young man's distinguished face, noting with pleasure the long, severe scholar's nose, brown eyes heavy with learning, sensitive yet ascetic lips, and a certain, almost hollow quality of the dark cheeks. He gazed around at shelves upon shelves of books and let out a soft, contented sigh.

When Leo's eyes fell upon the cards, he counted six spread out in Salzman's hand.

'So few?' he asked in disappointment.

'You wouldn't believe me how much cards I got in my office,' Salzman replied. 'The drawers are already filled to the top, so I keep them now in a barrel, but is every girl good for a new rabbi?'

Leo blushed at this, regretting all he had revealed of himself in a curriculum vitae he had sent to Salzman. He had thought it best to acquaint him with his strict standards and specifications, but in having done so, felt he had told the marriage broker more than was absolutely necessary.

He hesitantly inquired, 'Do you keep photographs of your clients on file?'

'First comes family, amount of dowry, also what kind promises,' Salzman replied, unbuttoning his tight coat and settling himself in the chair. 'After comes pictures, rabbi.'

'Call me Mr Finkle. I'm not yet a rabbi.'

Salzman said he would, but instead called him doctor, which he changed to rabbi when Leo was not listening too attentively.

Salzman adjusted his horn-rimmed spectacles, gently cleared his throat and read in an eager voice the contents of the top card:

'Sophie P. Twenty-four years. Widow one year. No children. Educated high school and two years college. Father promises eight thousand dollars. Has wonderful wholesale business. Also real estate. On the mother's side comes teachers, also one actor. Well known on Second Avenue.'

Leo gazed up in surprise. 'Did you say a widow?'

'A widow don't mean spoiled, rabbi. She lived with her husband maybe four months. He was a sick boy she made a mistake to marry him.'

'Marrying a widow has never entered my mind.'

'This is because you have no experience. A widow, especially if she is young and healthy like this girl, is a wonderful person to marry. She will be thankful to you the rest of her life. Believe me, if I was looking now for a bride, I would marry a widow.'

Leo reflected, then shook his head.

Salzman hunched his shoulders in an almost imperceptible gesture of disappointment. He placed the card down on the wooden table and began to read another:

'Lily H. High school teacher. Regular. Not a substitute. Has savings and new Dodge car. Lived in Paris one year. Father is successful dentist thirty-five years. Interested in professional man. Well Americanized family. Wonderful opportunity.

'I knew her personally,' said Salzman. 'I wish you could see this girl. She is a doll. Also very intelligent. All day you could talk to her about books and theyater and what not. She also knows current events.'

'I don't believe you mentioned her age?'

'Her age?' Salzman said, raising his brows. 'Her age is thirty-two years.'

Leo said after a while, 'I'm afraid that seems a little too old.'

Salzman let out a laugh. 'So how old are you, rabbi?'

'Twenty-seven.'

'So what is the difference, tell me, between twenty-seven and thirty-two? My own wife is seven years older than me. So what did I suffer? – Nothing. If Rothschild's a daughter wants to marry you, would you say on account of her age, no?'

'Yes,' Leo said dryly.

Salzman shook off the no in the yes. 'Five years don't mean a thing. I give you my word that when you will live with her for one week you will forget her age. What does it mean five years – that she lived more and knows more than somebody who is younger? On this girl, God bless her, years are not wasted. Each one that it comes makes better the bargain.'

'What subject does she teach in high school?'

'Languages. If you heard the way she speaks French, you

will think it is music. I am in the business twenty-five years, and I recommend her with my whole heart. Believe me, I know what I'm talking, rabbi.'

'What's on the next card?' Leo said abruptly.

Salzman reluctantly turned up the third card:

'Ruth K. Nineteen years. Honour student. Father offers thirteen thousand cash to the right bridegroom. He is a medical doctor. Stomach specialist with marvellous practice. Brother-in-law owns own garment business. Particular people.'

Salzman looked as if he had read his trump card.

'Did you say nineteen?' Leo asked with interest.

'On the dot.'

'Is she attractive?' He blushed. 'Pretty?'

Salzman kissed his finger tips. 'A little doll. On this I give you my word. Let me call the father tonight and you will see what means pretty.'

But Leo was troubled. 'You're sure she's that young?'

'This I am positive. The father will show you the birth certificate.'

'Are you positive there isn't something wrong with her?' Leo insisted.

'Who says there is wrong?'

'I don't understand why an American girl her age should go to a marriage broker.'

A smile spread over Salzman's face.

'So for the same reason you went, she comes.'

Leo flushed. 'I am pressed for time.'

Salzman, realizing he had been tactless, quickly explained. 'The father came, not her. He wants she should have the best, so he looks around himself. When we will locate the right boy he will introduce him and encourage. This makes a better marriage than if a young girl without experience takes for herself. I don't have to tell you this.'

'But don't you think this young girl believes in love?' Leo spoke uneasily.

Salzman was about to guffaw but caught himself and

said soberly. 'Love comes with the right person, not before.'

Leo parted dry lips but did not speak. Noticing that Salzman had snatched a glance at the next card, he cleverly asked, 'How is her health?'

'Perfect,' Salzman said, breathing with difficulty. 'Of course, she is a little lame on her right foot from an auto accident that it happened to her when she was twelve years, but nobody notices on account she is so brilliant and also beautiful.'

Leo got up heavily and went to the window. He felt curiously bitter and upbraided himself for having called in the marriage broker. Finally, he shook his head.

'Why not?' Salzman persisted, the pitch of his voice rising.

'Because I detest stomach specialists.'

'So what do you care what is his business? After you marry her do you need him? Who says he must come every Friday night in your house?'

Ashamed of the way the talk was going, Leo dismissed Salzman, who went home with heavy, melancholy eyes.

Though he had felt only relief at the marriage broker's departure, Leo was in low spirits the next day. He explained it as arising from Salzman's failure to produce a suitable bride for him. He did not care for his type of clientele. But when Leo found himself hesitating whether to seek out another matchmaker, one more polished than Pinye, he wondered if it could be – his protestations to the contrary, and although he honoured his father and mother – that he did not, in essence, care for the matchmaking institution? This thought he quickly put out of mind yet found himself still upset. All day he ran around in the woods – missed an important appointment, forgot to give out his laundry, walked out of a Broadway cafeteria without paying and had to run back with the ticket in his hand; had even not recognized his landlady in the street when she passed with a friend and courteously called out, 'A good evening to you, Doctor Finkle.' By nightfall, however, he had regained sufficient calm to sink his nose into a book and there found peace from his thoughts.

Almost at once there came a knock on the door. Before Leo could say enter, Salzman, commercial cupid, was standing in the room. His face was grey and meagre, his expression hungry, and he looked as if he would expire on his feet. Yet the marriage broker managed, by some trick of the muscles, to display a broad smile.

'So good evening. I am invited?'

Leo nodded, disturbed to see him again, yet unwilling to ask the man to leave.

Beaming still, Salzman laid his portfolio on the table. 'Rabbi, I got for you tonight good news.'

'I've asked you not to call me rabbi. I'm still a student.'

'Your worries are finished. I have for you a first-class bride.'

'Leave me in peace concerning this subject.' Leo pretended lack of interest.

'The world will dance at your wedding.'

'Please, Mr Salzman, no more.'

'But first must come back my strength,' Salzman said weakly. He fumbled with the portfolio straps and took out of the leather case an oily paper bag, from which he extracted a hard, seeded roll and a small, smoked white fish. With a quick motion of his hand he stripped the fish out of its skin and began ravenously to chew. 'All day in a rush,' he muttered.

Leo watched him eat.

'A sliced tomato you have maybe?' Salzman hesitantly inquired.

'No.'

The marriage broker shut his eyes and ate. When he had finished he carefully cleaned up the crumbs and rolled up the remains of the fish, in the paper bag. His spectacled eyes roamed the room until he discovered, amid some piles of books, a one-burner gas stove. Lifting his hat he humbly asked, 'A glass tea you got, rabbi?'

Conscience-stricken, Leo rose and brewed the tea. He served it with a chunk of lemon and two cubes of lump sugar, delighting Salzman.

After he had drunk his tea, Salzman's strength and good spirits were restored.

'So tell me, rabbi,' he said amiably, 'you considered some more the three clients I mentioned yesterday?'

'There was no need to consider.'

'Why not?'

'None of them suits me.'

'What then suits you?'

Leo let it pass because he could give only a confused answer.

Without waiting for a reply, Salzman asked, 'You remember this girl I talked to you – the high school teacher?'

'Age thirty-two?'

But, surprisingly, Salzman's face lit in a smile. 'Age twenty-nine.'

Leo shot him a look. 'Reduced from thirty-two?'

'A mistake,' Salzman avowed. 'I talked today with the dentist. He took me to his safety deposit box and showed me the birth certificate. She was twenty-nine last August. They made her a party in the mountains where she went for her vacation. When her father spoke to me the first time I forgot to write the age and I told you thirty-two, but now I remember this was a different client, a widow.'

'The same one you told me about? I thought she was twenty-four?'

'A different. Am I responsible that the world is filled with widows?'

'No, but I'm not interested in them, nor for that matter, in school teachers.'

Salzman pulled his clasped hands to his breast. Looking at the ceiling he devoutly exclaimed, 'Yiddishe kinder, what can I say to somebody that he is not interested in high school teachers? So what then you are interested?'

Leo flushed but controlled himself.

'In what else will you be interested,' Salzman went on, 'if you not interested in this fine girl that she speaks four languages and has personally in the bank ten thousand dollars? Also her father guarantees further twelve thousand. Also she has a new car, wonderful clothes, talks on all subjects, and she will give you a first-class home and children. How near do we come in our life to paradise?'

'If she's so wonderful, why wasn't she married ten years ago?'

'Why?' said Salzman with a heavy laugh. 'Why? Because she is *partikiler*. This is why. She wants the *best*.'

Leo was silent, amused at how he had entangled himself. But Salzman had aroused his interest in Lily H., and he began seriously to consider calling on her. When the marriage broker observed how intently Leo's mind was at work on the facts he had supplied, he felt certain they would soon come to an agreement.

Late Saturday afternoon, conscious of Salzman, Leo Finkle walked with Lily Hirschorn along Riverside Drive. He walked briskly and erectly, wearing with distinction the black fedora he had that morning taken with trepidation out of the dusty hat box on his closet shelf, and the heavy black Saturday coat he had thoroughly whisked clean. Leo also owned a walking stick, a present from a distant relative, but quickly put temptation aside and did not use it. Lily, petite and not unpretty, had on something signifying the approach of spring. She was *au courant*, animatedly, with all sorts of subjects, and he weighed her words and found her surprisingly sound – score another for Salzman, whom he uneasily sensed to be somewhere around, hiding perhaps high in a tree along the street, flashing the lady signals with a pocket mirror; or perhaps a cloven-hoofed Pan, piping nuptial ditties as he danced his invisible way before them, strewing wild buds on the walk and purple grapes in their path, symbolizing fruit of a union, though there was of course still none.

Lily startled Leo by remarking, 'I was thinking of Mr Salzman, a curious figure, wouldn't you say?'

Not certain what to answer, he nodded.

She bravely went on, blushing, 'I for one am grateful for his introducing us. Aren't you?'

He courteously replied, 'I am.'

'I mean,' she said with a little laugh – and it was all in good taste, or at least gave the effect of being not in bad – 'do you mind that we came together so?'

He was not displeased with her honesty, recognizing that she meant to set the relationship aright, and understanding that it took a certain amount of experience in life, and courage, to want to do it quite that way. One had to have some sort of past to make that kind of beginning.

He said that he did not mind. Salzman's function was traditional and honourable – valuable for what it might achieve, which, he pointed out, was frequently nothing.

Lily agreed with a sigh. They walked on for a while and she said after a long silence, again with a nervous laugh, 'Would you mind if I asked you something a little bit personal? Frankly, I find the subject fascinating.' Although Leo shrugged, she went on half embarrassedly, 'How was it that you came to your calling? I mean was it a sudden passionate inspiration?'

Leo, after a time, slowly replied, 'I was always interested in the Law.'

'You saw revealed in it the presence of the Highest?'

He nodded and changed the subject. 'I understand that you spent a little time in Paris, Miss Hirschorn?'

'Oh, did Mr Salzman tell you, Rabbi Finkle?' Leo winced but she went on, 'It was ages ago and almost forgotten. I remember I had to return for my sister's wedding.'

And Lily would not be put off. 'When,' she asked in a trembly voice, 'did you become enamoured of God?'

He stared at her. Then it came to him that she was talking not about Leo Finkle, but of a total stranger, some mystical figure, perhaps even passionate prophet that Salzman had dreamed up for her – no relation to the living or dead. Leo trembled with rage and weakness. The trickster had obviously sold her a bill of goods, just as he had him, who'd expected to become acquainted with a young lady of twenty-nine, only to behold, the moment he laid eyes upon her strained and anxious face, a woman past thirty-five and ageing rapidly. Only his self control had kept him this long in her presence.

'I am not,' he said gravely, 'a talented religious person,' and in seeking words to go on, found himself possessed by shame and fear. 'I think,' he said in a strained manner, 'that I came to God not because I loved Him, but because I did not.'

This confession he spoke harshly because its unexpectedness shook him.

Lily wilted. Leo saw a profusion of loaves of bread go flying like ducks high over his head, not unlike the winged loaves by which he had counted himself to sleep last night. Mercifully, then, it snowed, which he would not put past Salzman's machinations.

He was infuriated with the marriage broker and swore he would throw him out of the room the minute he reappeared. But Salzman did not come that night, and when Leo's anger had subsided, an unaccountable despair grew in its place. At first he thought this was caused by his disappointment in Lily, but before long it became evident that he had involved himself with Salzman without a true knowledge of his own intent. He gradually realized – with an emptiness that seized him with six hands – that he had called in the broker to find him a bride because he was incapable of doing it himself. This terrifying insight he had derived as a result of his meeting and conversation with Lily Hirschorn. Her probing questions had somehow irritated him into revealing – to himself more than her – the true nature of his relationship to God, and from that it had come upon him, with shocking force, that apart from his parents, he had never loved anyone. Or perhaps it went the other way, that he did not love God so well as he might, because he had not loved man. It seemed to Leo that his whole life stood starkly revealed and he saw himself for the first time as he truly was – unloved and loveless. This bitter but somehow not fully unexpected revelation brought him to a point of panic, controlled only by extraordinary effort. He covered his face with his hands and cried.

The week that followed was the worst of his life. He did not eat and lost weight. His beard darkened and grew ragged. He stopped attending seminars and almost never opened a book. He seriously considered leaving the Yeshivah, although he was deeply troubled at the thought of the loss of all his years of study – saw them like pages torn from a book, strewn over the city – and at the devastating effect of this decision upon his parents. But he had lived without knowledge of himself, and never in the Five Books and all the Commentaries – *mea culpa* – had the truth been revealed to him. He did not know where to turn, and in all this desolating loneliness there was no *to whom*, although he often thought of Lily but not once could bring himself to go downstairs and make the call. He became touchy and irritable, especially with his landlady, who asked him all manner of personal questions; on the other hand, sensing his own disagreeableness, he waylaid her on the stairs and apologized abjectly, until mortified, she ran from him. Out of this, however, he drew the consolation that he was a Jew and that a Jew suffered. But gradually, as the long and terrible week drew to a close, he regained his composure and some idea of purpose in life : to go on as planned. Although he was imperfect, the ideal was not. As for his quest of a bride, the thought of continuing afflicted him with anxiety and heartburn, yet perhaps with this new knowledge of himself he would be more successful than in the past. Perhaps love would now come to him and a bride to that love. And for this sanctified seeking who needed a Salzman?

The marriage broker, a skeleton with haunted eyes, returned that very night. He looked, withal, the picture of frustrated expectancy – as if he had steadfastly waited the week at Miss Lily Hirschorn's side for a telephone call that never came.

Casually coughing, Salzman came immediately to the point : 'So how did you like her?'

Leo's anger rose and he could not refrain from chiding the matchmaker : 'Why did you lie to me, Salzman?'

Salzman's pale face went dead white, the world had snowed on him.

'Did you not state that she was twenty-nine?' Leo insisted.

'I give you my word –'

'She was thirty-five, if a day. At *least* thirty-five.'

'Of this don't be too sure. Her father told me –'

'Never mind. The worst of it was that you lied to her.'

'How did I lie to her, tell me?'

'You told her things about me that weren't true. You made me out to be more, consequently less than I am. She had in mind a totally different person, a sort of semi-mystical Wonder Rabbi.'

'All I said, you was a religious man.'

'I can imagine.'

Salzman sighed. 'This is my weakness that I have,' he confessed. 'My wife says to me I shouldn't be a salesman, but when I have two fine people that they would be wonderful to be married, I am so happy that I talk too much.' He smiled wanly. 'This is why Salzman is a poor man.'

Leo's anger left him. 'Well, Salzman, I'm afraid that's all.'

The marriage broker fastened hungry eyes on him.

'You don't want any more a bride?'

'I do,' said Leo, 'but I have decided to seek her in a different way. I am no longer interested in an arranged marriage. To be frank, I now admit the necessity of pre-marital love. That is, I want to be in love with the one I marry.'

'Love?' said Salzman, astounded. After a moment he remarked, 'For us, our love is our life, not for the ladies. In the ghetto they –'

'I know, I know,' said Leo. 'I've thought of it often. Love, I have said to myself, should be a by-product of living and worship rather than its own end. Yet for myself I find it necessary to establish the level of my need and fulfill it.'

Salzman shrugged but answered, 'Listen, rabbi, if you want love, this I can find for you also. I have such beautiful clients that you will love them the minute your eyes will see them.'

Leo smiled unhappily. 'I'm afraid you don't understand.'

But Salzman hastily unstrapped his portfolio and withdrew a manila packet from it.

'Pictures,' he said, quickly laying the envelope on the table.

Leo called after him to take the pictures away, but as if on the wings of the wind, Salzman had disappeared.

March came. Leo had returned to his regular routine. Although he felt not quite himself yet – lacked energy – he was making plans for a more active social life. Of course it would cost something, but he was an expert in cutting corners; and when there were no corners left he would make circles rounder. All the while Salzman's pictures had lain on the table, gathering dust. Occasionally as Leo sat studying, or enjoying a cup of tea, his eyes fell on the manila envelope, but he never opened it.

The days went by and no social life to speak of developed with a member of the opposite sex – it was difficult, given the circumstances of his situation. One morning Leo toiled up the stairs to his room and stared out the window at the city. Although the day was bright his view of it was dark. For some time he watched the people in the street below hurrying along and then turned with a heavy heart to his little room. On the table was the packet. With a sudden relentless gesture he tore it open. For a half-hour he stood by the table in a state of excitement, examining the photographs of the ladies Salzman had included. Finally, with a deep sigh he put them down. There were six, of varying degrees of attractiveness, but look at them long enough and they all became Lily Hirschorn : all past their prime, all starved behind bright smiles, not a true personality in the lot. Life, despite their frantic yoohooings, had passed them by; they were pictures in a brief-case that stank of fish. After a while, however, as Leo attempted to return the photographs into the envelope, he found in it another, a snapshot of the type taken by a machine for a quarter. He gazed at it a moment and let out a cry.

Her face deeply moved him. Why, he could at first not say. It gave him the impression of youth – spring flowers, yet age – a sense of having been used to the bone, wasted; this came from the eyes, which were hauntingly familiar, yet absolutely strange. He had a vivid impression that he had met her before,

but try as he might he could not place her although he could
almost recall her name, as if he had read it in her own handwriting. No, this couldn't be; he would have remembered her.
It was not, he affirmed, that she had an extraordinary beauty
– no, though her face was attractive enough; it was that
something about her moved him. Feature for feature, even
some of the ladies of the photographs could do better; but she
leaped forth to his heart – had *lived*, or wanted to – more than
just wanted, perhaps regretted how she had lived – had somehow deeply suffered : it could be seen in the depths of those
reluctant eyes, and from the way the light enclosed and shone
from her, and within her, opening realms of possibility : this
was her own. Her he desired. His head ached and eyes nar-
rowed with the intensity of his gazing, then as if an obscure
fog had blown up in the mind, he experienced fear of her and
was aware that he had received an impression, somehow, of
evil. He shuddered, saying softly, it is thus with us all. Leo
brewed some tea in a small pot and sat sipping it without
sugar, to calm himself. But before he had finished drinking,
again with excitement he examined the face and found it
good : good for Leo Finkle. Only such a one could understand
him and help him seek whatever he was seeking. She might,
perhaps, love him. How she had happened to be among the
discards in Salzman's barrel he could never guess, but he knew
he must urgently go find her.

Leo rushed downstairs, grabbed up the Bronx telephone
book and searched for Salzman's home address. He was not
listed, nor was his office. Neither was he in the Manhattan
book. But Leo remembered having written down the address
on a slip of paper after he had read Salzman's advertisement in
the 'personals' column of the *Forward*. He ran up to his room
and tore through his papers, without luck. It was exasperat-
ing. Just when he needed the matchmaker he was nowhere
to be found. Fortunately Leo remembered to look in his wallet.
There on a card he found his name written and a Bronx address. No phone number was listed, the reason – Leo now recalled – he had originally communicated with Salzman by

letter. He got on his coat, put a hat on over his skull cap and hurried to the subway station. All the way to the far end of the Bronx he sat on the edge of his seat. He was more than once tempted to take out the picture and see if the girl's face was as he remembered it, but he refrained, allowing the snapshot to remain in his inside coat pocket, content to have her so close. When the train pulled into the station he was waiting at the door and bolted out. He quickly located the street Salzman had advertised.

The building he sought was less than a block from the subway, but it was not an office building, nor even a loft, nor a store in which one could rent office space. It was a very old tenement house. Leo found Salzman's name in pencil on a soiled tag under the bell and climbed three dark flights to his apartment. When he knocked, the door was opened by a thin, asthmatic, grey-haired woman, in felt slippers.

'Yes?' she said, expecting nothing. She listened without listening. He could have sworn he had seen her, too, before but knew it was an illusion.

'Salzman – does he live here? Pinye Salzman,' he said, 'the matchmaker?'

She stared at him a long minute. 'Of course.'

He felt embarrassed. 'Is he in?'

'No.' Her mouth, though left open, offered nothing more.

'The matter is urgent. Can you tell me where his office is?'

'In the air.' She pointed upward.

'You mean he has no office?' Leo asked.

'In his socks.'

He peered into the apartment. It was sunless and dingy, one large room divided by a half-open curtain, beyond which he could see a sagging metal bed. The near side of a room was crowded with rickety chairs, old bureaus, a three-legged table, racks of cooking utensils, and all the apparatus of a kitchen. But there was no sign of Salzman or his magic barrel, probably also a fragment of the imagination. An odour of frying fish made Leo weak to the knees.

'Where is he?' he insisted. 'I've got to see your husband.'

At length she answered, 'So who knows where he is? Every time he thinks a new thought he runs to a different place. Go home, he will find you.'

'Tell him Leo Finkle.'

She gave no sign she had heard.

He walked downstairs, depressed.

But Salzman, breathless, stood waiting at his door.

Leo was astounded and overjoyed. 'How did you get here before me?'

'I rushed.'

'Come inside.'

They entered. Leo fixed tea, and a sardine sandwich for Salzman. As they were drinking he reached behind him for the packet of pictures and handed them to the marriage broker.

Salzman put down his glass and said expectantly, 'You found somebody you like?'

'Not among these.'

The marriage broker turned away.

'Here is the one I want.' Leo held forth the snapshot.

Salzman slipped on his glasses and took the picture into his trembling hand. He turned ghastly and let out a groan.

'What's the matter?' cried Leo.

'Excuse me. Was an accident this picture. She isn't for you.'

Salzman frantically shoved the manila packet into his portfolio. He thrust the snapshot into his pocket and fled down the stairs.

Leo, after momentary paralysis, gave chase and cornered the marriage broker in the vestibule. The landlady made hysterical outcries but neither of them listened.

'Give me back the picture, Salzman.'

'No.' The pain in his eyes was terrible.

'Tell me who she is then.'

'This I can't tell you. Excuse me.'

He made to depart, but Leo, forgetting himself, seized the matchmaker by his tight coat and shook him frenziedly.

'Please,' sighed Salzman. '*Please*.'

Leo ashamedly let him go. 'Tell me who she is,' he begged. 'It's very important for me to know.'

'She is not for you. She is a wild one – wild, without shame. This is not a bride for a rabbi.'

'What do you mean wild?'

'Like an animal. Like a dog. For her to be poor was a sin. This is why to me she is dead now.'

'In God's name, what do you mean?'

'Her I can't introduce to you,' Salzman cried.

'Why are you so excited?'

'Why, he asks,' Salzman said, bursting into tears. 'This is my baby, my Stella, she should burn in hell.'

Leo hurried up to bed and hid under the covers. Under the covers he thought his life through. Although he soon fell asleep he could not sleep her out of his mind. He woke, beating his breast. Though he prayed to be rid of her, his prayers went unanswered. Through days of torment he endlessly struggled not to love her; fearing success, he escaped it. He then concluded to convert her to goodness, himself to God. The idea alternately nauseated and exalted him.

He perhaps did not know that he had come to a final decision until he encountered Salzman in a Broadway cafeteria. He was sitting alone at a rear table, sucking the bony remains of a fish. The marriage broker appeared haggard, and transparent to the point of vanishing.

Salzman looked up at first without recognizing him. Leo had grown a pointed beard and his eyes were weighted with wisdom.

'Salzman,' he said, 'love has at last come to my heart.'

'Who can love from a picture?' mocked the marriage broker.

'It is not impossible.'

'If you can love her, then you can love anybody. Let me show you some new clients that they just sent me their photographs. One is a little doll.'

'Just her I want,' Leo murmured.

'Don't be a fool, doctor. Don't bother with her.'

'Put me in touch with her, Salzman,' Leo said humbly. 'Perhaps I can be of service.'

Salzman had stopped eating and Leo understood with emotion that it was now arranged.

Leaving the cafeteria, he was, however, afflicted by a tormenting suspicion that Salzman had planned it all to happen this way.

Leo was informed by letter that she would meet him on a certain corner, and she was there one spring night, waiting under a street lamp. He appeared, carrying a small bouquet of violets and rosebuds. Stella stood by the lamp post, smoking. She wore white with red shoes, which fitted his expectations, although in a troubled moment he had imagined the dress red, and only the shoes white. She waited uneasily and shyly. From afar he saw that her eyes – clearly her father's – were filled with desperate innocence. He pictured, in her, his own redemption. Violins and lit candles revolved in the sky. Leo ran forward with flowers outthrust.

Around the corner, Salzman, leaning against a wall, chanted prayers for the dead.

More About Penguins
and Pelicans

For further information about books available from
Penguins please write to Dept EP, Penguin Books Ltd,
Harmondsworth, Middlesex UB7 ODA.

In the U.S.A.: For a complete list of books available
from Penguins in the United States write to Dept CS,
Penguin Books, 625 Madison Avenue, New York,
New York 10022.

In Canada: For a complete list of books available from
Penguins in Canada write to Penguin Books Canada Ltd,
2801 John Street, Markham, Ontario L3R 1B4.

In Australia: For a complete list of books available
from Penguins in Australia write to the Marketing
Department, Penguin Books Australia Ltd, P.O. Box 257,
Ringwood, Victoria 3134.

Bernard Malamud in Penguins

Dubin's Lives

A moving tale of love and marriage – a profound and comic novel by Bernard Malamud, master of the joys and surprises of fiction.

In William Dubin – a middle-aged, successful biographer seeking love, increased accomplishment and his secret self – the author has created one of his best characters; his novel is a compassionate and wry tragi-comedy of how a man lives by discipline, love, honour, fidelity and his passion for work. *Dubin's Lives* confirms what Alfred Kazin has said about Bernard Malamud: that there is no living writer who 'comes so close to the bone of human feeling, who makes one feel so keenly the enigmatic quality of life'.

'Certainly Malamud's best novel since *The Assistant*. Possibly, it is the best he has written of all' – *New York Times*

Also published:

The Assistant

The Fixer

Idiots First

The Magic Barrel

The Natural

A New Life

Pictures of Fidelman

The Tenants

Isaac Bashevis Singer in Penguins

The Magician of Lublin

He could tell jokes, perform tricks, pick locks, shell peas
with his toes, dance on the tightrope and turn somersaults
on the high wire. He owned a fine house and had a
lovely wife, Esther, who was devoted to him. He looked
ten years younger than he was, and to help sweeten his
travels there were delightful ladies. Life was good.
But Yasha was destined to find God and to discover faith,
and there was no middle road.

The Manor
and
The Estate

Isaac Bashevis Singer's acclaimed two-volume epic which
portrays, through the story of the Jacoby family,
the evolution of Europe and its Jewish community from
feudal traditions into the modern world.

'There is a massive authority in Singer's works, and
resonance to his characters, that place him among the
the really important living writers' – *Listener*

Also published:
A Crown of Feathers
Enemies: A Love Story
The Family Moskat
A Friend of Kafka and Other Stories
In My Father's Court
Passions and Other Stories
Satan in Goray
The Séance and Other Stories
The Slave